Chapter 1

"DARREL? I MEAN MIKE! What are you doing here in the middle of the night?" I called out to the contractor next door to Donut Hearts at three in the morning on my first day back on the job. The contractor had gone by Darrel when I'd first met him, but now everyone referred to him as Mike, and evidently that had been the name he'd used with everyone else before he'd gone to work for Gabby on rebuilding ReNEWed next door to my shop. What I had to wonder was if he had tried going by his middle name in order to duck his past. I wasn't sure about his rationale, but I knew that I was going to have a hard time adjusting to the change. His truck was parked in front of the construction site for ReNEWed, but I hadn't seen him since Jake and I had gotten back into town after our trip to Parsons Pond. Emma and Sharon had wanted a few extra days to run the shop together so they could both accumulate more money, and since Eloise Sandler had just paid Jake handsomely for his service while we had been looking for her son, I had agreed, but now I was itching to get back to work.

I could see a light on in the shell of the building, which at that point appeared to be mostly stud walls covered by some kind of plastic wrap. It wasn't transparent, but I could see a shape near one of the windows through the translucent material. He *had* to have heard me; I was standing within twenty feet of him.

"Mike!" I called out again.

There was still no response.

I decided to walk up the wooden gangplank that led from the red clay soil in front of the building site into the new construction. Was it possible that Mike had fallen asleep standing up?

I doubted it.

I was afraid what it might mean the moment he hadn't reacted to me calling out his name, but I had to know what was happening before I called anyone else.

I walked through the makeshift door, not much more than a slit in the plastic, and quickly moved to the area where I'd seen the man's silhouette outlined earlier.

Using the flashlight app on my cell phone, I lit up the space where he was standing.

Except he *wasn't*, at least not of his own accord.

It appeared that someone had used a nail gun to secure the contractor to the surrounding wood studs at his sleeves and his blue jean pants legs. As I moved closer to get a better look at his face, I could see that there was a massive amount of blood coming from his forehead and trickling down into his eyes. My hand shook as I reached out to search for a pulse I figured I wouldn't be able to find.

But to my surprise, his heart was still beating.

Mike Masters was still alive!

After dialing 911, I snapped out orders like a drill sergeant. "I need an ambulance at ReNEWed right now!" I barked.

"ReNEWed burned down," the dispatcher said dryly.

"Okay then, at the site where they're rebuilding it," I clarified.

"Was there a construction accident at *this* time of night?" the man asked. "I'm new, and I think I'm supposed to tell the EMTs what's going on when I call them."

We were wasting precious seconds that Mike Masters probably didn't have a great supply of left. "Tell them it appears to be blunt-force trauma and possible puncture wounds as well," I said as I noticed that at least one of the nails must have nicked the skin as it had been shot through his pants leg.

"Yeah, I can do that. Who are you?"

"Suzanne Hart," I said rapidly. "Tell them to hurry," I added as I ended the call.

It was less than two minutes later that I heard the ambulance siren and the police one following close behind it. I'd taken a few photos of the contractor and the general scene with my cell phone more out of habit than anything else, and then I'd searched for more signs of life, possibly even consciousness, but Masters didn't give me any indication that he even knew I was there.

The paramedics cut Mike Masters's clothes off of him and pulled out the lone nail that had pierced his skin as Chief of Police Stephen Grant joined us.

"What happened here?" he asked the crew curtly. "Why did you pull him down?"

"We're trying to save his life," the young woman said. "That trumps your investigation."

He shrugged. "What about you, Suzanne? Have you touched anything?"

"Just his neck when I was looking for a pulse. I just got here. I saw him outlined from outside the donut shop and came over to investigate. That's when I found him pinned to the wall like some kind of butterfly and called 911. It's Mike Masters, in case you two haven't met," I added lamely.

"We've met," Chief Grant said absently as he took in the scene.

"Professionally or personally?" I asked him.

"I barely knew the man, Suzanne," he said.

"Chief, we need you to hold the stretcher still for us for a second," one of the paramedics said.

Stephen Grant did as they asked, and the EMTs gently lowered the contractor's body onto the gurney.

"Is he still alive?" the police chief asked them.

"Barely," one of them said as they hurriedly wheeled Masters toward the makeshift door. She looked over at me as she added, "If she hadn't come along when she did, he wouldn't have had a chance."

I didn't even know how to react to that. In truth, I was feeling kind of numbed by the whole thing. No matter how many victims of violent crime I had run across in my life, I never seemed to get used to it. In some ways, finding Mike Masters still alive was as unnerving in its own way if not more. I could still feel the ghost of that weak pulse at my fingertips even though he was on his way to the hospital.

"Suzanne, are you going to be around this morning? I'd like to see you after you get back to the donut shop."

"Get back? Where am I going?" I asked him.

He pointed to my shirt. "I thought you might want to change." Evidently when I'd leaned across the contractor to check for the man's pulse, I must have gotten some of his blood on me. Head wounds were notoriously messy, and this one had left its mark on me.

"This isn't going to interfere with me making donuts today, is it?" I asked the police chief.

"No, the crime scene is next door to your shop. I need to take a formal statement from you on how you found him, but there's no reason I can see that you shouldn't open Donut Hearts as usual."

"Chief, there's nothing at all that is usual about finding a man pinned to the wall like some kind of science exhibit," I said, shivering a little at the thought of it. I looked down at the exposed plywood flooring below where he'd been unceremoniously mounted and saw that some blood had pooled there. How much had he lost while he'd been there waiting for me to find him? I fervently hoped that I'd gotten there in time.

"You know what I mean," he said.

"I'll be back in twenty minutes," I told him. That would still give me time to make both raised and drop donuts, though I might have to push things a bit. Still, I was a seasoned pro, and it would take more than finding Mike Masters to throw me off my donutmaking game completely.

"It takes you twenty minutes to change your clothes?" he asked me with a frown.

"You'd better believe that I'm going to take a shower, too," I told him. I wasn't sure how hard or long I'd have to scrub to feel clean again, but I was going to take as much time as I could spare to find out.

"Got it," he said, and then two of his deputies showed up.

"Oh, by the way. I took a few snapshots with my phone when I first got here, just in case. I'll forward them to you if you'd like," I said as I took my cell phone out and did as I'd promised.

"Thanks. I appreciate that," he said, clearly happy to have at least some record of what I'd found. My pictures might have lacked the clarity and thoroughness of what his people could do, but I figured that something was better than nothing. At least that was the way I looked at it.

"You're welcome. I'll be back soon," I said as I headed to my Jeep. I hesitated a moment before I left, though. "Let me know if anything changes in his status, would you?"

"You bet," the chief said.

"Thanks." I felt a little bit responsible for the man, even though I hadn't been a big fan of his the few times we'd interacted before I'd left town. He'd been brash and bossy, and from what I heard, he and Gabby had been dating while he'd been working for her. It had been enough to cause concern in both Jake's and Momma's eyes, and I knew their instincts combined were better than mine alone.

Clearly someone had a strong reason to hate the man enough to do what they'd done.

I was going to try to stay out of it, though.

I'd just about had my fill of investigating crimes for a while, and I was planning to take a sabbatical from my sleuthing if it was at all possible.

Later, thinking back on that promise I'd made to myself, I thought of one of my favorite sayings, four simple words that seemed to sum up my life.

Man plans, God laughs.

Chapter 2

"WHAT ARE YOU DOING back home so soon?" Jake asked me as I got out of the shower. I'd crept around trying to be as quiet as I could, but evidently something I'd done had woken him, even though I'd used my old bathroom upstairs to clean up.

"I found Mike Masters pinned to a stud wall at ReNEWed when I got to the donut shop," I told him. "Go back to sleep. There's nothing you can do."

Ignoring my advice, he sat up in bed instead. "Was he dead?"

"No, I found a pulse, so I called 911. I'm not sure what his condition is at the moment, but Chief Grant promised to keep me up to date."

Jake got out of bed and hugged me. I didn't think I needed it until my husband wrapped his arms around me. The moment that happened, the tension seemed to flow out of me, and I felt myself drawing strength from him. Ours was a symbiotic relationship, and I'd propped him up on occasion myself, but at the moment, I needed to feed off of his strength and calmness. After what had to have been nearly a full minute, I pulled away.

"Thanks. I needed that more than I can tell you."

"You know where to come if you need any more. There's plenty more where that came from," he said as he reached for his pants.

"You don't have to get dressed. I'll be fine at the donut shop by myself." As I said it, it occurred to me that he wasn't planning on going to work with me. Jake was a retired state police investigator. Of course he'd want to see the crime scene for himself. "Strike that. You want to talk to Chief Grant, don't you?"

"Why not? I'm awake anyway," he said with a shrug. "I might as well make use of the time and see if I can lend a hand, off the record and on the house, of course."

I knew better than to try to talk him out of it. "Do you want to ride over with me?"

"Why not?" he asked as he pulled on his socks and shoes. After grabbing a shirt, he followed me out the door, buttoning it as he walked. We were in a hurry, but that still didn't keep him from getting his weapon and strapping the shoulder holster on before adding a windbreaker to his ensemble.

"Do you think the chief will be okay with you just showing up?" I asked him as we walked out into the darkness toward my Jeep.

"If he isn't, I'll come back here," Jake said with a shrug, "but I doubt he'll run me off."

"I doubt it, too," I admitted.

After the short drive down Springs Avenue to the donut shop, I saw that my normal early-morning parking space was taken by a police squad car. I found a spot a little farther down, and Jake stopped and kissed me before going up the ramp to ReNEWed. "I'll be over later."

"I'll be here," I said. I unlocked the front door of Donut Hearts and started flipping on the usual switches, bringing the coffee pot and the fryer to life along with a small light up front and the entire complement of them in the kitchen. I decided to make an extra morning batch of coffee for the crew working next door, but that wouldn't be a problem, and as I started mixing the cake donuts I started with every day, I decided to do a double batch so I could give them away as well. It didn't cost me much as far as supplies were concerned, and it was a nice gesture to help the police officers working in the middle of the night, trying to keep the rest of us safe.

As I worked, I wondered who had taken such a personal dislike to Mike Masters. It was one thing to club a man in the face, but quite another to then pin him to the wall with a nail gun. Did Gabby know, I wondered? If not, I'd have to tell her myself, something I wasn't looking forward to. Gabby Williams could be volatile on her best days, and this was most assuredly not going to be one of those. Someone had attacked her contractor—and, if the rumors were to be believed, her boyfriend—and they had made quite a statement in how they'd mistreated him. She was going to be upset, which was putting it mildly to be sure, and there weren't many folks in April Springs who could calm her down. I thought I might be one of them, but this would surely test that theory.

With the first run of batter mixed, I started dropping plain cake donuts into the oil the moment it came to temperature, and before long, I had four trays of plain glazed cake donuts ready to go. I was going to have to mix another batch of cake donut batter later, but it shouldn't be too much of a problem. After all, I could always fry them while the yeast donuts were going through their second resting phase. I would also have to cut my usual break short, but at least for this morning it would be well worth it.

I mixed the ingredients for the raised donuts in the large stand mixer, and as soon as the dough was ready, I pulled out the massive mixing hook and covered the bowl in order to let it rest before the next step. After that, it was easy enough to box up the donuts I'd made earlier, transfer the majority of the coffee into a large urn, and then start another pot while I was gone. Grabbing a cart from the back, I put the urn, the donuts, a sleeve of cups with lids, plates and napkins on it and went next door.

"Suzanne, I'll be glad to pay you for these," Chief Grant said as he took another donut and I refilled his coffee cup.

"Sorry, but somebody's already beaten you to it," I lied. I was going to eat the cost of supplies and time myself, but the chief didn't have to know the details. He was a stickler for always paying his way, but there were times and circumstances where that didn't fit into my plans, so I decided to do what I wanted to anyway.

He looked surprised. "Who knows about this already?"

"Please. This is April Springs," I reminded him, neatly sidestepping his question. "You're covered."

"At least tell me who I need to thank," he said craftily.

"I would, but the contributor insisted that it be anonymous," I replied.

Jake came out of the building site and said with a smile, "I was hoping you'd do that."

"It's the least I can do," I said.

"She won't tell me who's covering the cost of this spread," Chief Grant protested. "Do you want to take a swing at it?"

"Me? You're kidding, right? I'm not about to try to get her to break her donutmaker confidentiality agreement," he said as he grabbed a cup of coffee and a donut.

"There's no such thing," the police chief protested.

"Try telling *her* that," Jake said. "You'd have more luck convincing a stone to talk, though. If I were you, I'd just say thank you and move on."

"Thank you," Chief Grant told me.

"You're welcome. I'll pass on your gratitude to my benefactor."

"I'm sure you will," he said with a wry smile.

"Have you been able to make any progress?" I asked.

Jake deferred to the chief, which I thought was a classy thing to do, especially since I'd asked him the question and not Chief Grant.

"I just heard from the hospital. Masters is stable, but he's still unconscious," he told me guardedly. "That's not common knowledge, so I'd appreciate it if you'd keep that to yourself."

"Will do," I said. "What about the crime scene?" I followed up as I gestured toward the building. After all, maybe my treats would garner me a little more goodwill than I'd used up so far.

"Everything that would hold a print that might be relevant was wiped clean, including the nail gun," he said with a shrug. "Unless someone happened to see something while it was happening, we're going to have to rely on Masters talking, and so far, that hasn't happened."

"Do they know just how bad it is?" I asked.

"If they do, they aren't telling me," the chief said as he put his cup down. "I'm going back in. Thanks again for the donuts and coffee." He then turned to Jake. "Are you coming?"

"I'm right behind you," he said as he followed the police chief in, hesitating only long enough to wink at me.

I was cleaning up the cart and getting ready to push it back next door when I heard a car door slam ten feet behind me.

Gabby Williams rushed toward the building. I knew that I had to stop her, even if it meant tackling her before she could get inside.

That dried pool of blood would surely send her over the edge, assuming she wasn't there already.

"Hang on a second, Gabby," I said as I stepped in front of her.

"Get out of my way, Suzanne!" she said angrily.

"He's at the hospital!" I said, slapping her with my words. "You should be there, not here!" It was a jolting thing to say, and I was sure that it was just as hard for her to hear, but I had to get her attention.

"I tried," she said, nearly bursting into tears. "They wouldn't let me see him." As she said it, I moved forward, and she practically fell into my arms, sobbing.

"It's going to be okay, Gabby," I said soothingly as I stroked her back gently.

"You don't know that. Nobody does," she said as she choked out the words.

"That's true, I don't, but he's in good hands, and when I found him, he was still hanging on."

"What did he look like when you saw him?" she asked me as she started to pull away.

"He was alive," I replied, trying to skirt the issue.

"I've had enough of that from the hospital. Tell me what you saw. I want to know everything," she added as she pulled back and stared into my eyes. "Give me the truth."

"Somebody nailed him to the wall, Gabby," I said, not trying to sugarcoat it, but struggling to give the woman exactly what she'd asked for. I figured she at least deserved that from someone. "He caught a nail in the leg, but the worst of it was the wound to his head."

"They hit him with something hard," she said, her voice flattening out as though she was being controlled by someone else. "It was a hammer, they told me."

"I didn't know what it was, but there was a lot of blood."

"Could you see the wound itself?" she asked me.

"No." I was relieved to be able to tell her that at least.

"Why would someone do that to him?"

"Gabby, I have no idea. I don't know him all that well, and we've been gone this past week. I figure you'd know the answer to that better than I would."

Gabby wiped the tears from her eyes, and then she said, "If I didn't know that it wasn't true, I'd say that *I* was the most likely person to do it, Suzanne."

"What?" I asked incredulously. "Why would *you* do something like that?"

"I found out last night that he'd been cheating me and cheating *on* me all at the same time. It turns out that he was padding his bill to cover up the money, my money, he was spending on some little tramp in Union Square."

"What did you do when you found out?" I asked her. "Gabby, tell me you didn't threaten him publicly."

"I wish I could, but I can't," she said, and then the woman I'd known for so many years as strong and fierce nearly broke down for the second time in ten minutes right in front of me. She pointed to the table in front of Donut Hearts we kept out there for our al fresco diners. "After I found out, I came here, and I waited for the crew to leave last night. I was about to go in when he came out. Mike was talking on the phone to her while he was in my building! Can you believe the nerve?"

My ex-husband had cheated on me in a pretty overt way too, so I could easily believe it. I didn't think it was appropriate to bring that up just then, though. "How did you find out about it?"

"I got an anonymous tip that said he was cheating on me in more ways than one," she said. "At first I didn't believe it, but when I checked the bills he gave me versus the actual invoices, I saw that at least that much of it was true, and probably the rest of it, too. He must have bragged about how brilliant he was to someone who felt bad for me and decided to let me know what was going on right under my nose."

"How did they get in contact with you? Was it a man or a woman? Did you get their number? Tell me everything you can about them."

Gabby shrugged. "I don't have the slightest idea who it could have been. There was a note in my mailbox yesterday. I didn't talk to anybody."

"Let me at least see it," I told her. It appeared that Gabby was in trouble. How much trouble was yet to be determined, but I couldn't help her if I didn't have all of the facts as well as the evidence at my disposal.

"I tore it up and threw it away," she said angrily. "What did you think I would do, frame it and hang it on the wall?"

"That was a bit rash. Where did you toss it?"

"I put it in my trash can," she said.

"We need to go recover that note," I told her.

"It's too late," she said, clearly regretting her behavior in hindsight. "The trash people came by five minutes after I tossed it. Why is that so important, Suzanne? It won't take back anything that happened over the last twelve hours."

"No, but it might just help keep you out of jail," I told her.

Gabby looked shocked by the implication. "*Jail*? I didn't do that awful thing to him, Suzanne. I was angry with Mike, but I didn't attack him."

"I don't think you did for one second," I told her, "but you have to know that you're going to be a suspect. I'm willing to bet that there was at least one witness to your confrontation. This is April Springs, after all, and I'm willing to bet that *somebody's* going to come forward. As a matter of fact, I would say that you can count on it. What did Masters say when you confronted him?"

"I didn't give him a chance to smooth things over with me, if that's what you're asking. He was too good at lying to me."

"How did you end it with him, Gabby?"

"I told him that if I ever saw his face around here again, I'd kill him," she admitted.

It was even worse than I'd imagined.

"Then you'd better hope that he wakes up soon and tells the police who really attacked him," I said. "Otherwise, I'm not sure what is going to happen to you."

Chapter 3

"I KNEW SOMEDAY MY TEMPER would be my downfall," Gabby said soberly. "I don't know what got into me."

"It's perfectly understandable given the circumstances," I said softly. "Don't be so hard on yourself. He hurt you, Gabby. It's only natural for you to lash out."

"Did you ever threaten Max?" Gabby asked me.

"No," I admitted. "I did suggest that he sleep with one eye open for a while, but that was more of a general suggestion than a direct threat. I wasn't the only person in town who was unhappy with him when he cheated on me with Darlene."

"I can understand that, but the two of you were married. Mike was probably just exploiting me all along. He was younger and probably too handsome for me, even if he did have a mean way about him."

"You can't know for a fact that he was using you," I told her just as my timer went off.

"You've got to go. I'm sorry I kept you," Gabby said as she shivered a bit. It was warm during the days but could still be a little chilly at nights, which provided weather I was usually perfectly happy with since the humidity hadn't visited us in full force yet. It was clear by Gabby's apologetic tone that what had happened to her former boyfriend and contractor had shaken her to her very core, and I couldn't abandon her just because my donuts needed some attention.

"Come inside and keep me company while I work," I told her.

"Suzanne, you don't have to coddle me."

"I know that," I said. "Come on. It'll be fun."

She shrugged. "Well, I don't suppose there's one chance in a million of me getting back to sleep after this, so I might as well. Fine. Are you sure I won't be in the way?"

There was room in my kitchen for two people, if just barely. "You'll be more than that. You'll be welcome. It'll be fun."

"Let's not get too carried away," she said a bit drily, and I knew that there was probably hope for her yet.

After I got Gabby situated on a stool in one corner of the kitchen, I punched down the yeast dough and got started on the next phase. Once that task was accomplished, I went back to my cake recipe so I could offer my customers both types of the donuts they loved. The cops and Jake had eaten more than half the cake donuts I'd offered them earlier, and I clearly didn't have enough to limp through the rest of the day without making another batch. As I worked, Gabby sipped some coffee and nibbled on one of the cake donuts I'd made earlier.

"I thought Emma still worked with you," she said as she looked around the kitchen.

"She does, but once a week, I still solo here. It gives me a chance to stay connected to the place on a personal level."

Gabby frowned for a moment before she spoke. "So then I probably shouldn't offer to help with these dishes, is that what you're saying?"

"I didn't invite you here to work. You're my guest," I replied, neatly skirting her offer. It wasn't that I was all gung ho on doing everything myself, especially since I was making a double batch of cake donuts, but I didn't feel right putting her to work.

"Honestly, Suzanne, I need something to do. I can't just sit here like a pretty, pretty princess and watch you work." She grabbed an apron, and before I could say another word, Gabby started filling up one side of the sink with warm, soapy water.

"If you're sure you don't mind, I really would appreciate it," I said.

"If I didn't want to, do you honestly think I'd be doing it?" she asked me with the hint of a frown.

"No, ma'am. You've always struck me as the type of woman who didn't do *anything* she didn't want to," I said with a smile to soften the blow of my words.

"It's true enough. By the way, thank you," she said as she got to work.

"You're welcome, but why thank me?"

"For not tiptoeing around me," she answered.

"Gabby, I haven't done that in years," I said with a soft laugh. There had been a time long ago when I'd done exactly that, but something had changed in our relationship since then. Now whenever I needed to tell her the cold, stark truth about something, I took a deep breath and just did it. Gabby might not have always liked the frank way I talked to her, but she respected it, and that was what counted.

"No, you haven't," she said. "So, what are we going to do?"

Her question confused me for a second. "I thought it was fairly clear. I'm making donuts and you're washing dishes. Why, has something changed?"

"I mean about Mike," she said firmly.

"I'm not sure there's anything we *can* do about him until he wakes up," I said. I didn't add the last bit, "or else he doesn't," but she knew it was implied.

"We can't wait for that to happen," Gabby said. "My reputation is getting shredded every second he's out cold, and we both know it."

"What do you suggest?"

"We can figure out what happened ourselves," Gabby said.

I would have sworn in a court of law that it was just a coincidence when I dropped the empty tray I'd been about to use for the freshly made cake donuts.

At least I hoped that was what it was.

"What's the matter? Don't you think I could help you solve this case?" she asked me, just daring me to admit otherwise.

"Gabby, I have no doubt that you'd be an asset," I said, stretching the truth a little. "There's only one problem. You're too close to it."

"What do you mean? Who *else* is better qualified to help you dig into Mike Masters's life than I am? Name one person, Suzanne."

"That's the problem, though," I said. "Folks would clam up if you started asking them about Mike, and we both know it." There were more reasons than that, but for the moment, it had to be enough.

I hoped.

Gabby looked frustrated. "I suppose you'll ask Grace to help you."

I pulled a batch of cake donuts out of the hot oil and let them drain a second before I doused them with glaze. "Who says I'm digging into this?"

"You can't turn your back on me now, Suzanne, not when I need you."

Blast it all, she clearly knew how to push my buttons. Had Momma been giving her lessons? I could fight her on it, but we both knew that I'd eventually give in, so what was the point in putting up even a futile resistance? "Fine, I'll see if Grace is free."

"But if she's not, I can help you, right?" Gabby asked. "Jake can't do it. He's working with Chief Grant—who, by the way, is not a big fan of Mike's either."

"Why not?" I asked, hoping to distract her.

"They just seemed to dislike each other from the very first time they met. When I think about it, his instincts were clearly better than mine," Gabby said. "I just want to know that I'm at least number two on your list."

"I can't say that," I told her. "I've worked with Momma and Phillip before with great success, and they are both distanced enough from the heart of the case to allow some objectivity."

"They can't help you. Didn't you know?" she asked me, clearly curious about something.

"Know what?" I asked, troubled by the sudden turn in our conversation.

"They're going on a trip out of town in a few hours," Gabby explained.

"No, I haven't heard anything about it, but you'd better believe that I'm about to," I said as I pulled out my phone and dialed my mother's phone number. I didn't care what time it was. She and I needed to talk.

"I hear you're going on a trip," I told her when she answered my call right away. Given the hour of the morning, Momma was surprisingly chipper and alert. "If I'd known about it beforehand, I could have thrown you a farewell party."

"Suzanne, I was going to come by the shop and tell you when you opened this morning," Momma said calmly. "No one is supposed to know about our trip, so I'm curious as to who told you."

"Does that really matter?" I asked, refusing to throw my source under the bus. "Where exactly are you going?"

"We're heading to Charleston to see an old friend of mine," Momma said.

"You're going to the coast of South Carolina?" I asked her. I'd just recently been enticed with a trip to the North Carolina Outer Banks only to find that I'd be thirty miles short of it, so I wasn't in the mood to hear that my mother was going to get the vacation I'd been expecting.

"No, the other Charleston, the one in West Virginia," she said.

"Who do you know who lives there?" I asked her.

"My old college roommate moved back to take care of her mother, and she's got a massive home on the banks of the Kanawha River. It's supposed to be quite lovely," she said.

"How long are you going to be gone?" I asked. At least she wasn't going to the beach, though I'd heard that West Virginia's capital city was nice enough in its own right.

"It shouldn't be more than three or four days," Momma said. "Phillip insisted that we stop by the shop this morning and tell you ourselves in person."

"Did he by any chance hope to get some donuts for the trip while he was here?" I asked, smiling despite my pique. My stepfather enjoyed my donuts whenever my mother allowed him to indulge.

"I may have offered to let him buy a few on the way out of town," Momma admitted.

"I'll make up a box of his favorites on the house," I said.

"We can pay our own way, young lady. You know that you can't afford to give your treats away."

"Funny you should say that, because I gave away half a batch of cake donuts and a full urn of coffee to the police not ninety minutes ago," I admitted.

"What happened?" she asked.

I stepped out into the dining area before I answered her question. I hadn't wanted Gabby to overhear my conversation with my mother, especially since I figured the assault on Mike Masters would come up in our chat. In a soft voice I said, "Someone beat Mike Masters and then nailed him to the stud walls at ReNEWed," I told her.

"How ghastly," she said. "You were the one who found the body, weren't you?"

"What makes you just assume that's what happened?" I asked her.

"You didn't deny it, did you?" she responded, the angst clear in her voice. "Was he dead?"

"No, the last I heard, he was hanging on, but it's still touch and go."

"Gabby must be devastated," Momma said. "I should check in on her on my way out of town."

"Funny you should say that. As a matter of fact, you can see her when you stop by Donut Hearts," I told her.

"She's *there*?" Momma asked incredulously.

"She is. As a matter of fact, at this very moment, she's up to her elbows in warm, soapy water," I admitted.

"You put her to *work*?" Momma asked incredulously.

"She volunteered," I said in my own defense. "It seems to be helping her get her mind off what happened. Apparently she and Mike had a fight last night, so I'm going to help her figure out what happened in case he doesn't wake up soon."

"Suzanne, I don't have to tell you that Gabby would be a liability to your investigation, do I? Is Jake available to help you?"

"He's working with Chief Grant," I said.

"Then we'll cancel our trip and stay here," Momma said decisively.

"I appreciate the offer, but I'm going to ask Grace to help," I told her. "You don't have to change your plans on my account."

"I thought her boss was some kind of horrible taskmaster," Momma said.

"She was, but then she got promoted, so now she's someone else's headache," I told her. "Grace called me not long after we got home from Parsons Pond and told me all about it. I'll be fine, Momma."

"You're sure?"

"I'm positive," I said as Gabby came out of the kitchen.

"Suzanne, your timer just went off."

"Gotta go, Momma," I said. "See you later."

"Good-bye, Suzanne," she replied as I was hanging up on her.

"Is everything okay with Dot?" Gabby asked as we walked back into the kitchen together.

"She's fine. She sends her love," I added. Though strictly speaking, Momma had done nothing of the sort, I knew that she would have if I'd given her the time.

"Your mother is one classy lady," Gabby said as I saw to my next step in the yeast donutmaking process.

"I think so, too," I said. "She's coming by at six when I open."

"I'll be gone by then," Gabby said with a shrug. "I have no desire to be on public display after what happened this morning."

"I get it," I said, "but is being home going to be any better? You can always stay back in the kitchen here if you'd like."

"Suzanne Hart, I've never run away from a fight—or the truth for that matter—in my life. I have nothing to be ashamed of!"

"I never said that you did!" I snapped right back.

After a moment, Gabby looked at me sheepishly. "Sorry. I'm a bit on edge at the moment."

"You don't have to apologize to me," I said in a much kinder voice. "Now, while we're waiting for something else to happen, let's both see if a little work won't make the time go by faster."

Chapter 4

"HERE WE ARE, AS PROMISED," Momma said as I opened the doors to Donut Hearts at six a.m.

"Come on in," I replied as I stepped aside and let them in. My minor frustration with Momma was now long forgotten. "You two sure are getting an early start."

"You don't know the half of it. She's had me up half the night packing," Phillip explained. "The only reason I agreed to go at all was if I could have some of your donuts for the drive."

"Here you go," I told him as I slid a full box of a dozen donuts across the counter to him. I'd put in ten of Phillip's favorites and two of my mother's. I suspected I might have been overly generous with her portion, but hey, I was feeling magnanimous, at least at the moment.

"Suzanne Hart, we never agreed on a dozen," Momma protested.

"They aren't *all* for the trip up," I said. "What if Charleston doesn't have any donuts that are as good as mine?"

"I'm sure they have something perfectly acceptable, but if not, we'll manage to muddle through somehow anyway," Momma said.

"Dot, let's just take them all in the spirit they were offered. After all, we don't want to put Suzanne to any extra work pulling out donuts and shifting things around on her display shelves," Phillip protested as he opened the box and spied the array of treats inside.

"What work would that be, exactly?" Momma asked him.

"Think about it. She'd have to unpack these, get a new box, pick a few for that one, and then she'd have to restock the rejects, if she can even sell them as new at this point. Once they make it into a box, aren't they done for the day, Suzanne?"

I didn't have a set policy on that since this exact situation had never come up, but I wasn't about to throw my stepfather under the bus for loving my donuts too much. "It's true, Momma. I went to a lot of work making these. You can't expect me to just pitch them into the garbage, can you?"

It was a bald-faced lie, and what was more, the three of us knew it. Gabby hadn't wanted to see anyone, even my mother, so she'd asked to stay in the kitchen once I opened, which was fine by me. I'd hidden back there myself a time or two over the years.

"Fine," Momma said, "but you get no dessert tonight, Phillip."

He grinned at her. "Who needs dessert? I've got Suzanne's donuts." He winked at me. "Thanks for the treats."

"You bet. Call me when you get there, okay?" I asked my mother.

"I will," she agreed. "Stay safe, Suzanne."

"I'll do my best," I said.

Momma lowered her voice. "Where is Gabby, by the way?"

"She's in back," I said in an equally soft tone. "I'd call her out here, but she's not really up for company."

"I can certainly understand that, given the circumstances. Give her my love."

"I already did," I answered as I stepped around the counter and hugged them both before they left.

Once they were gone and I'd waited on a handful of customers, the kitchen door opened tentatively, and Gabby's head peeked out. "Is the coast clear?"

I walked over to her. "No, I've got three customers here eating their donuts. Why, do you need to leave?"

"No, I just wanted to see if you had any more dishes that needed to be washed," she said.

"You're finished with those already?" I asked her. I was starting to feel guilty about drafting her into cleanup duty, but then I remembered that she'd insisted, so that eased my guilt at least a little.

"There's no reason washing dishes must be such a chore," she said. "I even put everything away where I thought it should go."

It took all that I had not to groan upon hearing that. Emma and I struggled constantly with "where things should go," at least in our own opinions. Where Gabby determined that to be was impossible to fathom, so I knew I'd be spending some time after she left getting things back to the way I liked them. My way might not have been the *best* way, but it worked for me, and hey, in the end, it was *my* donut shop, so I reserved the right to arrange it in whatever manner I saw fit. "Thanks," I said. "I appreciate that."

"You're welcome," she replied. As she finished the sentence, she ducked back into the kitchen as though something had frightened her. If it scared Gabby Williams, it would probably terrify me, so I grabbed the softball bat I kept under the counter for protection before I turned around.

It was just Chief Grant and Jake though, so I put the bat back where I'd stored it.

"Gentlemen, did you come by for seconds," I asked them brightly, "or do you have news for me?"

"There's nothing new to report," the chief said with a frown.

"About Mike Masters's condition or the attack on him?" I asked.

"Both. Neither. You know what I mean. You haven't by any chance seen Gabby Williams, have you? We've been looking all over town for her," the chief said.

I glanced at Jake, who just shrugged helplessly. It was clear this was the police chief's investigation, and my husband was there only by his indulgence. That left me in a quandary, though. Did I turn Gabby in, or should I keep her presence at the donut shop a secret? I decided my best course of action was to stall. "Why are you looking for her?"

"It's no big deal. I just have some questions for her," Chief Grant said.

"About what, exactly?" I pressed him further.

"Suzanne, I don't really have to justify why I'm looking for her to you," he snapped.

Jake cleared his throat, but he didn't say a word. The chief looked at him as though he'd just been slapped down, and the next thing he said was spoken with a great deal more civility. "I'm sorry. I didn't get much sleep last night, and I'm a little snippy. I need to find out why she threatened to kill Masters last night."

So I'd been right. Someone had overheard the confrontation after all. I was about to try to stall a bit more when the kitchen door opened and Gabby stepped out. Evidently she'd been eavesdropping the entire time.

"I'll tell you the truth, Chief," she said, "but not here."

"That's fine by me," Chief Grant said. "We can go to my office."

"Gabby, you shouldn't talk to him without a lawyer," I warned her as I stepped in front of her.

"That's ridiculous! I don't have anything to hide," she protested.

I didn't say a word, but I gave her a stern look that she couldn't misinterpret. "Fine," was all that she said as she walked out the door.

The chief paused a moment before he left. "You didn't have to do that, Suzanne," he said, almost as though I'd hurt his feelings by what I'd said.

"It's nothing personal, Chief," I answered. "I just know how this all must look to you."

"Hey, I've got an open mind," he said.

"I know that," I answered as I touched his arm and smiled hesitantly.

He answered it in kind. "Okay then." As he walked toward the door, he turned to my husband. "Coming, Jake?"

"I'm right behind you, Chief," he said as he winked at me once Chief Grant was past him.

I gave him a slight smile, and my dear husband returned it before he followed the others out the door.

I hated giving Stephen Grant a reason to think that I didn't trust him, but Gabby's life could be on the line, and that meant that all bets were off. I was going to do everything I could to protect my friend, even if it meant angering other people, including the police chief and even my husband. To be fair though, I got the distinct impression that Jake hadn't been all that unhappy with my suggestion to Gabby. He was a pro through and through, while our police chief was young and still growing into his job, though getting better at it every day.

After they were all gone, I turned back to the business at hand—at least for the moment—which was selling donuts, something that I was more than capable of doing. I just hoped that when I started my second task for the day—which was uncovering what had really happened to Mike Masters—I'd be just as suited for that as well.

Only time would tell, though.

Sam Graham from the gas station came in for two dozen donuts a little later, something he did every now and then.

"Who's watching the pumps if you're here, Sam?" I asked him.

"Haven't you heard? I have an intern now two days a week," Sam replied with a grin.

"An intern? At a gas station?" I asked him as I got his order together. "No offense, but is that really a thing?"

"Not until Stevie came along, it wasn't. It's kind of hilarious. I'm telling you, Stevie Marks could talk the ink off a postage stamp. He somehow convinced the guidance counselor at the high school that since he wants to be an entrepreneur when he graduates, he needs to work at as many jobs as he can to get the feel for them before he strikes out on his own," Sam said with a smile.

"You just watch, that kid is going to end up owning April Springs someday," I said.

"I think so, too. That's why I'm getting in good with him now," Sam answered. He was always happy, and I envied him his general sunny disposition. I was usually good-natured enough, but that man could give lessons on looking on the brighter side of life. That was why his sudden frown looked so out of character. "It's a real shame about what happened next door," Sam said.

"The word got out fast, didn't it?"

"Hey, *everybody* talks to me," Sam replied. "Running a gas station is like having your very own grapevine."

Here was a possible source of information that I hadn't even considered in the past. Could Sam join my list of folks I could tap? "Have you met Mike Masters?"

"Yep," Sam said briefly. "Drives a bright-red Tundra pickup. It might be a long-bed, but that thing's engine is only a four liter, if you can believe that. What were they thinking?"

"What's your opinion of the man?" I asked.

"Gabby could do better," he allowed.

"For a boyfriend or a builder?"

"Both," Sam said. "I saw him catting around with Regina Davis the other night, and with a gal from Union Square named Crispy or Crisco or something the night before that. As to his building abilities, I heard from a contractor who bid on the ReNEWed job that Masters was a crook. It wasn't sour grapes or anything, he said it matter-of-factly to me while he was filling up his F-350 Diesel." Clearly Sam associated the drivers who visited his gas station more with their vehicles than anything else, which I supposed made sense. I must be the Jeep Woman to him, and Jake was most likely just another truck guy.

"Do you have any idea who might have attacked him?" I asked as I gave him his change.

"I don't have a clue, but I know that I'd hate to be the one who had to make the list," he answered.

"Why is that?"

"I don't have enough paper," Sam said with a shrug. "Thanks for the grub."

"Don't eat them all at once," I replied with a smile.

"Why not? That's one of the joys of being a grown-up, isn't it? You can pretty much do whatever you want until you get married."

Sam was a confirmed bachelor, so I asked him, "Ever thought about taking the plunge yourself?"

"Sometimes," he said with that characteristic smile of his. "Then I find a dark corner and curl up into a ball until I get over it." He paused to smell the air in the donut shop, which definitely had a distinct aroma to it. "Might make an exception for a gal with her own donut shop, though."

I waved my wedding ring in his direction. "Sorry, but I'm already spoken for."

"It figures. All the best ones are," he said, laughing as he exited the shop.

That was interesting. Evidently Mike Masters hadn't been all that circumspect about his behavior, either on the job or on the town. That would certainly leave him open to the kind of attack he'd suffered, but if Sam was right, it would make my job a lot harder if the contractor didn't wake up soon and tell us exactly what had happened to him.

Chapter 5

I WAS ABOUT TO CLOSE up for the day when I saw Jake approaching. The second he walked into Donut Hearts, I hit him with a barrage of questions. "Is there any news about Mike Masters? How's Gabby doing? Did she take my advice and get an attorney?"

"She did," Jake said, answering my last question first.

"Well? What's going on?"

"She just left the police station," my husband explained. "Don't worry, she wasn't arrested. Chief Grant asked her not to leave town, though. She said she wasn't going anywhere, so for now, she should be okay."

"Jake, she didn't do it," I said.

"Suzanne, I know the woman is your friend, but the police are going to need more than just your word for it."

"Maybe *they* do, but my gut is good enough for me." I decided not to ask him if it was good enough for him, too. I didn't want to make things any more difficult for my husband than I had to. His instincts, developed after years as an investigator, weren't easy for him to ignore, and I knew it.

"I admire your loyalty to your friends," he said. "Anyway, I thought I'd pop by and tell you where things stand at the moment. No word on Masters as of yet."

"Does Stephen really think that Gabby could have done it?" I asked him.

"It's a possibility that he *has* to consider or he's not doing his job," Jake explained to me.

"I get that, but what does he *think*?"

"He's getting to be too good a cop to think *anything* without having more facts." Jake must have realized how harsh that sounded, because he quickly added, "We're just trying to get to the truth, Suzanne."

"I understand, but you should know Gabby's asked me to dig into this, and I told her that I would do it as a favor to a friend," I said.

He nodded. "I expect nothing less from you. Do you have a partner picked out yet? I'd help you myself, but I already promised the chief that I'd lend him a hand, unofficially of course. If you want me to drop out of his investigation and join yours, all you have to do is ask. I'm sure he'd understand."

"That's sweet of you to offer," I said as I touched his cheek lightly, "but he's expecting you to help him work this case, and I don't want you to have to go back on your word."

"Could Dot or Phillip pitch in?" he asked. I knew my husband didn't want me looking into anything criminal on my own, and I respected his position.

"They are on their way to West Virginia even as we speak, visiting Momma's old college roommate," I said.

Jake frowned. "With Grace's new boss being such a taskmaster, I'm assuming she can't help you, either."

"The woman got a big promotion, so I'm going to ask her as soon as I'm finished up here for the day," I explained. I hadn't had a chance to tell him the news yet about Grace's change in supervision.

"And if *she* can't do it for some reason?"

"Gabby offered to help," I told him, trying not to smile as I said it.

"Suzanne, you can't be seriously considering that," Jake said vehemently. "She would be the absolute *worst* choice, and you know it."

"Don't worry, that's what *I* told her when she offered to help me," I said, failing to hide my grin any longer.

"I hope you put it a little more delicately than that."

"Let's just say that she got the message," I answered.

"Maybe George could pitch in," Jake said, thinking aloud. "He's offered to help more than once lately, and you two used to work together before he got hurt."

That was true enough, but I wasn't about to risk our mayor's life again, not when he'd come so close to dying before doing something at my behest. "One way or the other, I'll figure it out."

"Do me a favor and call Grace right now," Jake said.

"Honestly, I'll be fine."

"Indulge me," he said firmly.

I started to protest again, but then I decided to give in. After all, he had my best interests at heart.

I got Grace on the second ring. "Where are you?"

"In the kitchen with the knife and Colonel Catsup," she said with a laugh.

"Are you sure that's not Mustard?" I asked.

"I'm pretty sure. Hang on and I'll ask him." She muted her phone for a few seconds and then came back. "He says his name is Catsup, and I have no reason not to believe him."

"Is there any chance you're working from home today?"

"As a matter of fact, that's exactly what I'm doing. I'm catching up on my paperwork. At least that's what's going to go on my worksheet I have to turn in every week."

"What are you *actually* doing?"

"Mostly just relishing my newly rediscovered freedom," she answered with another laugh. "It's amazing how good it feels."

"Do you have any interest in digging into an assault case with me?"

"What happened? Did someone attack you, Suzanne?" Suddenly there was no playfulness in her voice anymore.

"I'm fine, but someone hit Gabby Williams's ex-boyfriend/contractor in the head with a hammer and then nailed him to a stud wall at ReNEWed sometime late last night or early this morning."

She hesitated before she replied, no doubt taking it all in. "Is there any chance that *Gabby* did it? No, of course not. She asked you to find out what happened though, didn't she?"

"Yes, and I've agreed to help her."

"You said assault, so I'm assuming the man is still alive," Grace said.

"Hang on and let me double-check. Jake is right here." I put the phone against my chest and turned to my husband. "You said before that Masters was still alive, right?"

"Yes, as of ten minutes ago, anyway. He hasn't come out of it yet, though, and the doctors are starting to get worried about him."

I nodded and turned back to the phone. "He's alive, but for how much longer no one can say. Are you game?"

"I'm ready and able," she said. "I'll see you in fifteen minutes."

"I'll be at Donut Hearts," I told her.

"Of course you are. After all, where else would you be?" she asked. "Thanks for asking me to help you, Suzanne."

"Yours was the first name on my list," I told her, and then I hung up. "Grace is going to help me, so you're in the clear," I said.

"Suzanne, you know how much I love digging into these messes with you, but I already gave the chief my word."

"Don't apologize. I figure with both of us working on this case, we'll have it solved in no time."

"Do you really believe that?" he asked me.

"If it's wishful thinking, I'm okay with that," I told him.

"So am I," he said as his cell phone rang. "It's the chief."

"Take it," I said as I kissed him briefly and sent him on his way even as he was answering the call. I had some work to do at the shop before Grace got there, but at least I'd cut it close enough with my donut estimate that I didn't have that many to get rid of. Eight donuts wasn't bad, considering the fact that I'd made a double batch of cake donuts earlier. The report balanced to the penny, and I was waiting outside for Grace with the deposit bag on the table in front of me when she walked up.

"You're ready early," she accused me.

"What can I say? I'm efficient. Is your company car okay? They didn't take it back, did they?"

"It's all of a hundred yards here from my house, and I figured you'd want to drive us around in your Jeep," she said. "Besides, they're starting to pay pretty close attention to our mileage, so I may not be driving us around much for the time being. It's a change my former pain of a boss implemented, and it's probably going to take a month or two before I can start safely ignoring it again."

"I'm happy to drive," I said as I walked past my Jeep toward the Boxcar Grill.

"Okay," she said. "Are we going to go see Trish?"

"I haven't had lunch yet. How about you?" I asked her.

"I got up half an hour ago, so no, I haven't," she said with a smile. "If we're being technical, I haven't had breakfast, either. I decided to sleep in today, but hey, I've had a burger for breakfast before, and it didn't kill me."

"That's good to know," I said. "We're on completely different internal clocks, aren't we?"

"And yet it's never put a damper on our amazing friendship," she answered as we walked up the steps into the Boxcar Grill.

"It would take more than a clock to come between us," I agreed.

"Well, if it isn't the dynamic duo back together again," Trish Granger said as we walked into her diner. "I haven't seen you two hanging out lately."

"I got a pesky boss who insisted that I work forty hours a week, every week, if you can believe that," Grace explained with a hint of exasperation in her voice.

"Don't you just hate when that happens?" Trish asked. "Suzanne, when was the last time you worked a forty-hour week?"

"It hasn't been all that long ago, since I turned Donut Hearts over to Emma and Sharon two days a week," I admitted. "In the old days, it was more like fifty or sixty, but I've got it pared down to quite a bit less than that lately, and I have to say, I don't mind it one bit."

"Fair enough. Maybe I should take on an assistant manager, too," she said. "No, that wouldn't work. I'm too hands-on here. Oh well, I'll just dream of having spare time and leave it at that."

"Trish, we all know that you wouldn't know what to do with yourself if you had any free time on your hands," I told her with a smile.

"Maybe, but just think about what kind of trouble I could get into," she said mischievously.

"It makes me nervous just considering the possibilities," I told her.

"That's what makes it so much fun," she said.

Trish handed us a pair of menus, but one look at the specials board told me all I needed to know. "I'll have sweet tea, country-style steak, mashed potatoes and gravy, fried okra, and a roll on the side."

"I like a woman who knows what she wants," Trish said. "How about you?"

"That sounds good to me too," Grace said.

I had noticed that the diner owner had been looking at the partial box of donuts I had under one arm. I'd nearly forgotten all about them, so I put them on the counter and slid them across to her. "I had some leftovers."

"Sweet," she said as she put them under the counter. "Thanks."

"You bet," I answered. I'd been wondering what I was going to do with them. Sometimes I used spare donuts as bribes to get folks to talk to me, and sometimes I dropped them off at the church for the soup kitchen, but I also loved giving them away to my friends. There was something satisfying about putting a box of fresh donuts into someone else's hands who wasn't expecting it.

"Where do you want to sit?" I asked Grace as we walked into the relatively crowded dining area.

"There's a spot in back," she said, and we made our way there and claimed it before someone else could.

In ten minutes, there were no tables free, and some folks were starting to stand around, waiting for one to open up. I spotted Jenny Preston, owner of For The Birds, looking troubled. "Grace, there's Jenny, and she looks as though she has the weight of the world on her shoulders. Do you mind if I invite her over to join us?"

"That's fine with me. I'm a big fan of Jenny's too," she said, so when I got her attention, I waved her over to our table. She smiled slightly as she took the free seat. There was only one, since someone had borrowed the fourth for their table from us a minute earlier.

"What's going on, Jenny?" I asked her after she ordered. "Are you okay?"

"Haven't you heard the news?" she asked.

"About Mike Masters? Why? Has something happened to him?"

She looked at me oddly. "To be honest with you, Mike is the *last* thing on my mind at the moment. We had an argument yesterday, and I had to throw him out of my shop. How did *you* hear about that?"

"I hadn't," I admitted. "What were you talking about if it wasn't the contractor?"

"You first," she insisted.

"Somebody attacked Mike Masters at ReNEWed last night or early this morning. He's in bad shape."

Jenny slumped down into her seat even further. "I hadn't heard. I just admitted that I had a fight with the man and voilà, someone attacks him. Wow, could this day get any worse?"

"It's going to be okay," I said as I patted her hand.

"You shouldn't give it another thought. I've heard plenty of stories about the man since he started working in town, and I'm guessing that there's a *long* list of folks who had a beef with the man. What did you two fight about?" Grace asked her.

I wanted to know what Jenny had originally been talking about, but Grace's question was important, too. The storeowner frowned as she recounted, "He came in demanding to do a job for me, but it was one I didn't want done anymore, so we had some hard words."

"I'd be angry about that, too," Grace said. "What was the job?"

"Last month, I knew the shop was in trouble," Jenny admitted. "When the store beside mine gave up their lease, I thought I might be able to turn things around by knocking a door through the wall and expanding my shop. I know it was stupid in retrospect, but I was desperate. I called Masters after I got his name from a friend, and I got a quote on what it would cost. I never promised him anything, and an hour after he left, I realized how dumb it would be for me to pour good money after bad. I just left my accountant's office half an hour ago, and I've had to face some cold, hard facts. I can't keep the shop open anymore." She looked devastated by the news, and I couldn't blame her. I knew a lot of small businesses struggled, and hers was no exception. I'd wondered when she'd opened if there would be enough demand for a shop catering just to bird lovers in our little town, but I had kept that to myself. After all, other niche stores managed to make it through lean times. I had undergone a few rough patches myself over the years, and I sold treats, for goodness' sake.

"I'm so very sorry," I told her.

She shrugged. "It's just the icing on the cake of one bad decision after another. The truth is, you inspired me when you took your divorce settlement from Max and bought Donut Hearts, Suzanne. I thought I'd do the same thing, but it didn't work out for me as well as it did for you."

Wow, now I *really* felt bad about that. "I had no idea you were in that much trouble," I told her. "Are you sure there isn't anything you can do? If it would help, we could do an event where everyone who buys something at the shop gets a free donut. I'll supply them on the house. Maybe it will generate enough traffic to buy you a little time."

Jenny smiled, and there was nothing half measured about it. "Thanks, but it wouldn't help. No, I need to face facts. For The Birds turns out to indeed be for the birds."

"So, getting back to your earlier story, you turned Masters down, and it escalated into a fight?" Grace asked.

I hadn't had the heart to push her, but evidently my investigative partner had no such compunctions. Maybe it was because Grace had always worked for someone else. There was something particularly soul crushing about trying to turn a dream into reality and failing at it.

"I told him outright that it wasn't going to happen, and he started giving me the hardest sell I've ever gotten in my life. He told me that he'd get me the cheapest materials for the job and that he'd do it close to cost, but I had to give him a deposit, in cash, on the spot. The man reeked of desperation, so even if I'd still been considering it, that would have turned me off. I said, 'If I had that much cash on hand, I wouldn't be going broke.'"

"How did he react to your rejection?"

"He started screaming at me that I owed him the money and that he had to have it. I got out my pepper spray, and I honestly thought I was going to have to dose him to get him to leave. He finally took off, but not before knocking a display of wind chimes over and storming out."

"Wind chimes?" I asked.

"They feature different birds for the weights that hang down from the clapper," she explained. "They are what catch the wind and make the clapper move."

That was more than I really wanted to know about wind chimes, but I could tell that it gave her some comfort in sharing the information with us, so I wasn't going to push her on it. "Got it."

"I'm guessing that he talked to everyone he ever gave a quote to," Jenny said.

"Were there really that many?"

"You're kidding, right? He gave out business cards as though they were party favors. I'm surprised he didn't try to hit you up for a job, too," she said. "I'm guessing if you talk to anyone else near my shop, they'll tell you that he came by looking for some quick cash there, too."

"Why do you suppose he needed money so urgently?" Grace asked her.

"Who knows? Gambling? Drugs? It could have been anything."

Jenny's food arrived, and even though we had finished ours, I couldn't just leave her. "What are you going to do now?" I asked her.

"There's not much that I can do. I'm going to have a big sale, see if I can pay off my debts, and start over," she said as she took a bite. "At least this is tasty, so the day isn't a total wash."

"You're not going to open up another bird-themed shop, are you?" Grace asked her.

"No, not a chance. In fact, I think I'll go back to work for someone else. I'm through being the one with the headaches and the ulcers. Let someone else sweat the details."

"My offer stands. I can still make donuts for your close-out sale," I offered.

"You don't have to do that, Suzanne."

"I know that, but I want to. Please?" I had to do *something* to help her out, even though I knew that realistically, I hadn't had anything to do with her business's creation or its ultimate failure either, for that matter.

"If you're sure," she said. "I was thinking I might as well rip the Band-Aid off and get it over with. How does next Monday sound?"

"I'll be there," I said. "Emma can run Donut Hearts, and I'll spend the day serving donuts to your customers."

"I can drum up some advertising for it," Grace offered. "I have a friend who's really good at that sort of thing."

"I don't know what to say, ladies," she answered as she clearly fought an onslaught of tears.

"You don't have to say anything," I told her.

Trish approached us with a concerned look. "Is everything okay with lunch?"

"It's amazing," Jenny said.

"You just looked upset, so I thought I'd come over and check on you."

"I'm shutting down For The Birds." It seemed to help her to say it out loud. I hoped that I'd never have to say the same thing about Donut Hearts.

"We're doing a blowout next Monday to help her sell out her inventory," Grace said.

"That's a bit optimistic, isn't it?" Jenny asked.

"Not with the four of us behind it," Trish said.

"You're going to help, too?" she asked.

"What are friends for? We'll do hamburgers and hotdogs at the store. I'll even man the grill and leave Hilda here to fend for herself. We'll put whatever we make in your cash register."

"I just had a sudden burst of inspiration. I can cover your costs, and Suzanne's, too," Grace chimed in.

"You don't have to do that," I told her.

"That's the beauty of it, though. If I can hand out some lipstick samples, I can write it all off," Grace replied happily. "My not-so-brilliant-but-ever-so-painful boss ordered a ton of samples in a truly hideous shade, so why not give them away for a good cause? Come on, let's make this happen."

"Thank you all so much," Jenny muttered as she stood and raced to the restroom, no doubt to have herself a long-overdue cry.

Grace pulled out a twenty and handed it to Trish.

The diner owner studied the extended money without taking it. "Grace, I appreciate the gesture, but my expenses are going to be a lot more than this."

"I know that, you nit," my best friend said with a smile. "That should cover all three of our lunches." Grace turned to me. "Should we wait here for her to get back?"

"You two go on," Trish said. "I've got this."

"Thanks," I said. "Tell her we'll be in touch."

"You bet. It's a shame it's going to be for her closing, but we'll make sure she goes out with a bang."

"You bet we will. You're my kind of lady," I told Trish as I stood and hugged her.

"Coming from you, that's the nicest compliment I could get," she answered. "Now shoo."

"Yes, ma'am," we said in unison and walked out together.

Once we were back at my Jeep, Grace asked, "Is Jenny going to be okay?"

"Given time, I'm sure that she will be," I said. "I have faith in my friends. Thanks for pitching in and financing the entire event," I added.

"I'm just glad to be able to," she said. "I've been itching to use my promotion budget on something selfish, and this fits the bill perfectly."

"I hardly call helping a friend being selfish," I corrected her. Much like Gabby, Grace didn't want the world to know just how big her heart was, but I'd known it since we'd been kids.

"Whatever. That's my story, and I'm sticking to it," she answered. "Now, am I correct in assuming that we're going to go talk to Regina Davis?"

"You are," I said as we started driving.

I was going to do my best not to worry about Jenny until the "going out of business" sale. In the meantime, I had another job to do besides making donuts, one that might just mean the difference between freedom and jail for one of my dear friends.

Chapter 6

"WHAT DO YOU TWO WANT?" Regina asked when we walked into the office of the scrapyard. Her father, Garry, owned the place just outside of town, and she'd worked there ever since we'd all graduated from high school. Regina had a tendency of dressing like a tart all through school, and I could see that her taste in clothes hadn't changed all that much over the years. Her outfit might not have looked half bad if she'd still had the figure for it, but she was asking her clothes to do way too much of the work to make her look young and vibrant, which I assumed was what she was going for. Regina was a strong and solid girl with well-defined arms, and I wondered how much time she spent out in the scrapyard, tossing heavy chunks of metal around herself.

"Now Regina, is that any way to greet a pair of old friends?" Grace asked her sweetly.

"No, but then the three of us were *never* friends. You two were always too cool for me."

"*Me? Cool?* Ask anybody. I've never been cool a day in my life," I told her. "I wasn't a cheerleader, a jock, or even a brain. I never belonged to *any* of those groups."

"No, you did something cooler than that; you floated between them," Regina said. "Grace was always the *pretty* one, coasting on her good looks, but you managed to make friends with just about anybody you ever met."

I didn't know how to answer that, but Grace did it for me. "It's called being nice, and for your information, I never coasted a day in my life, but thanks for the compliment anyway. Regina, did you hear what happened to Mike Masters?"

It took her two seconds too long to answer the question. "Who?"

"Come on," I said in as friendly a voice as I could muster. "We know that you were seeing him, so there's no use pretending otherwise."

"Isn't he a little old for you, Regina?" Grace asked.

She shrugged. "Okay, I admit it. I've gone out with him a few times. Yeah, he's older than I am. So what? I don't know if you've noticed, but guys haven't exactly been beating down the door to date me the last few years. He was a laugh; that's all."

"We heard that it was more than that," Grace said. I didn't in fact know if that were true or not, but it was clear that Grace wanted to see how she reacted to the implication that they were more serious than she was letting on. "Aren't you concerned about him?"

"Why should I be?" she asked as she played with a large bandage on her left hand.

"What happened there?" I asked as I pointed to her injury.

"When you work in a scrapyard, you pick up some nicks and cuts along the way," she said as she tried to hide the bandage.

"Are you saying you didn't know that someone attacked Mike Masters last night and left him for dead at ReNEWed?"

Her face paled a bit. "Mike is *dead*?"

"No, at least not the last we heard. Whoever tried to get rid of him didn't quite succeed," I said. "We're trying to find out who attacked him."

Regina frowned. "I don't understand. If Mike's still alive, why don't you just *ask* him?"

"He's still unconscious," I admitted.

Did she seem a bit relieved by that particular bit of news? I couldn't honestly tell. The woman was hard to read; in fact, she always had been. "That's too bad, but I certainly didn't have anything to do with it. I'm sorry it happened, but I don't know why you're here."

"Regina, you were spotted with him a few nights ago," I told her in a sympathetic tone.

"We went out a few times, but he wasn't exactly my Mr. Right, you know? Not all of us are lucky enough to find guys that are willing to hang around for the long run. Hey, it even took *you* two tries before you got it right."

"Let's not make this personal, Regina," Grace said in my defense before I could form an answer.

"Don't you think coming to my workplace and asking me nosy questions is personal too, or does it not count if *you're* the ones prying into other people's lives? I know all about you two, playing detective. Why don't you drop it and let the real cops do their job."

"Are you trying to tell us that you don't care what happened to Mike Masters one way or the other?" Grace asked her pointedly. "That's cold, even for you."

Regina paused a moment before she answered. I could almost see the wheels turning in her mind. "I didn't mean for it to sound that way. Of course I'm not happy somebody attacked him, but I didn't do it, and to be honest with you, I have no idea who might have." After a moment, she added, "Then again, maybe I do. Did you know that he was seeing Gabby Williams? Maybe *she* went after him. He bragged about playing her for a fool, and if she found out, I could see her attacking him."

Unfortunately, it wasn't that far a leap to make for anyone else either, including the police. I thought it was impressive that Stephen Grant had showed such remarkable restraint by *not* locking her up, but then again, how long would he be able to put it off?

"You don't happen to have any jealous suitors, do you?" I asked her.

Regina laughed at the suggestion. "Believe me, nobody's going out of their way to defend my honor, if that's what you're asking me."

A loud voice suddenly came over the intercom. "Regina, I need you at the scales. Mullany's bringing in another load of scrap, and I want to make sure he doesn't mix any garbage in with it again this time."

"I'm on it, Pop," she said, and then she turned to us. "Sorry I can't hang around and have you accuse me of attacking a guy I dated a few times, but I've got work to do."

"We don't mind waiting," I said as pleasantly as I could.

"There's no reason for you to. I don't know anything about what happened to Mike," she said, dismissing us.

"If we think of anything else, we'll come back by and chat with you later," Grace said, ignoring her outright denial.

Regina wasn't happy about that prospect and was obviously about to reply when the radio blurted out again, "Come on, you need to move it, kid!"

"10-4," Regina said. As she walked to the door that led to the scales, she shot us a quick and unhappy look. "I didn't do it, and that's the truth. When Mike wakes up, he's going to tell you the same thing."

"Wow, some people never change, do they?" Grace asked me as we walked back out to my Jeep.

"I don't know. She seemed more vulnerable now than she did in school, if you ask me," I said.

"Did you see the arms on her, Suzanne? She looks as though she could easily have pinned the contractor against the wall with one hand."

"I'm talking about emotionally, though she does look strong physically," I agreed. "That doesn't mean that she attacked Mike Masters, though. The truth is that I kind of feel sorry for her."

"Yes, I get what you mean," Grace answered, softening her stance a bit. "Can you imagine being desperate enough to date Mike Masters if you weren't married to Jake?"

"Me? No way," I answered quickly. "How about you?"

"I can't even imagine the circumstances," Grace admitted, "even if I weren't seeing Stephen."

"She hasn't had the easiest life, you know," I said as we drove out of the parking lot. "Her mother ran off when she was in grade school, and her dad has been all that she's had ever since."

"I understand that, but we've both known kids with much tougher lives growing up, and they turned out just fine," Grace said. It was unlike her to be so uncharitable in earnest. Sure, we joked around a lot, but Grace usually had such a big heart.

"It's not like you to be so harsh with people, Grace. Why are you so upset with Regina?"

"She said I coasted!" Grace said. "Suzanne, do *you* think I sailed through school on my looks?" It was clear that Regina's comment had struck home about one of Grace's insecurities.

"Of course not," I said. "Certainly you were pretty, but you didn't use it as a club like some girls we went to school with did. Don't let her get to you."

Grace frowned. "High school *was* a long time ago, wasn't it? Maybe I just need to let it go."

"I know it's tough, believe me, but that's really the only thing you can do at this point in your life," I said. "What do you think about what Regina just told us?"

Grace paused a moment before answering. "She tried to lie to us right out of the gate about even knowing Mike Masters, let alone dating him, and that troubles me. Nobody pauses that long that many times when they're telling the truth. Do you think she was more serious about him than she claimed?"

"It's entirely possible," I said. "All I know is that we need to dig into her story harder. I thought I had it rough making donuts in the middle of the night while everyone else was sleeping, but at least I'm not usually injured at work. I wonder what really happened to her hand."

"She could have been telling the truth about that, because she really is around a ton of sharp objects all day long," Grace said. "It's amazing to me that she didn't have more Band-Aids on than she did."

"I guess," I said. "We need to head to Union Square and see if we can find Masters's other mystery date. What was her name again?"

"Crispy or Crisco is all we have to go on," Grace said with a shrug. "How on earth are we going to find *her*? It's not a lot to go on, is it?"

"No, but we have resources in Union Square that we can tap," I reminded her. "Surely at least one member of the DeAngelis clan has heard of this mystery woman."

Grace frowned. "I suppose."

"Don't you want to go see Angelica and her daughters?" I asked her as I headed toward Napoli's in Union Square.

"Of course I do. I just wish that we hadn't already had our lunch," she said.

"That's a fair point," I said, "but you know Angelica. She's not going to let us get out of there without feeding us at least a little something."

"That's what I'm counting on," Grace said with a smile.

We were in for a big surprise when we got to the restaurant, though. There was plenty of parking in front, but the place was clearly crowded, so I decided to head around back, where the mother and daughters parked during the workday. As I pulled my Jeep around the building, I saw a familiar face leaving the back of the restaurant with a silly grin on his face.

What on earth was he doing there in the middle of the day?

"Mr. Mayor, what are you doing out of your jurisdiction?" I asked George Morris as we approached him on foot after I'd parked my Jeep.

George Morris looked clearly startled by our presence, almost as though we'd caught him doing something he shouldn't have been doing. "Suzanne? Grace? What are you two doing here?"

"That was Suzanne's question for you, remember?" Grace asked him with a grin.

I looked closer and saw a smudge of red lipstick on his cheek. "Are you and Angelica dating by any chance, George?" I asked. I'd been prodding him for months to ask her out. Had he finally gotten up the courage to do so?

"Yes, but we're not telling anybody just yet," he said with a shrug. "We want to see where it's going before folks make a big deal of it. Can I trust you two to keep our secret?" he asked.

The teasing comment I'd been about to make suddenly died on my lips when I saw how earnest he was. "Of course you can," I told him. "For what it's worth, I hope it works out."

"So do I," Grace said.

"That makes four of us if you include Angelica," the mayor said. "I've got to run. I have a council meeting in forty-five minutes," he added.

"Hang on a second," I said as I took out my clean handkerchief and wiped the lipstick smudge off his cheek. "There, that's better."

"Thanks," he said sheepishly before getting into his truck and driving off.

Once he was gone, I turned to Grace. "As tempting as it's going to be for both of us, we can't let Angelica know that we just ran into George," I told her.

"That's probably the right thing to do, but it surely isn't going to be the easiest," Grace answered. "George and Angelica. Who would have thought it was even possible? I wonder what the girls think. Do they even know?"

"I can't imagine Angelica being able to hide it from them," I said, "and I'm sure they're all thrilled for their mother. She's been alone long enough, and so has George."

"He's a little old to start courting a woman like her though, isn't he?" Grace asked. "I was beginning to think that George was going to be a bachelor for life."

"Maybe he was just waiting for the right woman to come along," I said. I knew that our mayor had dated several nice women over the years, but none of the relationships had seemed to stick. Angelica was the total package though, and if the mayor had to end up with someone, he couldn't have done any better, at least as far as I was concerned. "Are you ready to go in and pretend that we didn't see a thing?"

"I'll try my best," Grace said, "but I'm not promising anything."

"Grace," I said.

"Okay, it'll be tough, but I'll be a good girl."

"That's the spirit," I said as I knocked on the back door and walked on in.

"Ladies, how long have you two been out there?" Angelica asked us the moment we entered the kitchen. She was a bit flushed, and there seemed to be an extra gleam in her eye. Or was it possible that was just my imagination?

"We just got here," I lied, and Grace nodded in agreement. "Angelica, do you have a second?"

"Seriously, Mom? You just got back from some mysterious errand, and now you're going to chat with our friends before you get to work?" Sophia, the youngest daughter, asked her mother with a smile.

"I was under the impression that you and your sisters had things under control here," she answered in mock severity. "Was I wrong?"

"No, ma'am, you got it right in one," Sophia said with a grin. "We're handling things."

"Excellent," Angelica said. She stepped closer to us and said softly, "They are amazing young women. I'm lucky to have them."

"I heard that," Sophia shouted.

"Get back to work," Angelica replied without looking at her. Sophia couldn't see her mother's smile, but we could.

One of the other daughters, Antonia, swatted her youngest sister playfully with a dish towel. "Where's that baked ziti I asked for?"

"Coming right up, sis," Sophia said.

"We don't want to keep you," I said, "but do you happen to know a woman named Crispy or Crisco who might have been dating a contractor named Mike Masters?"

"You're talking about Jillian Christie," Tianna said as she stood near the door. She must have been waiting tables with Antonia, and I hadn't even seen her come into the kitchen. Tianna had been estranged from the family for quite a while, but she'd been welcomed back into the fold when they'd finally worked things out. I knew it made Angelica happy to have all of her daughters at Napoli's again, and who could blame her?

"How do you happen to know her?" Angelica asked her oldest daughter.

"I went to school with her, remember?" she asked.

"Of course," Angelica answered, though it was clear that she had no distinct memory of the young woman in question.

"Tianna, do you know where we might find her?" I asked.

"She works at Sullivan's," she said.

"The tire store?" I asked.

"That's the one," she admitted. "I'm still waiting on two lasagnas and a chicken alfredo," she told her little sister.

"That's it. I'm stepping in," Angelica said as she grabbed an apron.

"I can do this, Mom," Sophia insisted.

Her mother ignored her. "Do I ever ask you for help when things are busy, or do you pitch in on your own without being asked?"

"I guess that's true enough," Sophia answered reluctantly.

"You know that it is," Angelica said as she dove into the work.

It was clear that they were too busy for our question-and-answer session. "We'd better leave you to it. It was good seeing you ladies."

"You two aren't going to stay and have a bite?" Angelica asked us, seemingly shocked that we would ever drop in without at least sampling something.

"Next time," I promised.

"Hold on one second," Tianna said as she approached us. In a gentle voice, she said, "Don't tell Jillian I sent you, okay?"

"Why? Is there bad blood between you?" Grace asked her softly.

Tianna shook her head. "No, that's not it at all. As a matter of fact, she's my best friend. The truth is that I've been worried about her lately. She's been dating older men, and not the nice kind, either. I've heard that Mike Masters didn't treat her well at all."

"How did they happen to meet? Was he getting tires at the shop?" I asked. I was always curious about what brought people together, maybe because my beginning with Jake had started out with a customer's murder. First meetings didn't get much odder than that.

"That's what she said. He has an office here in town, did you know that?"

"As a matter of fact, we didn't," I said as I turned to Grace. "Do you happen to know where it is?"

"It's in one of the strip malls over near Cheap Cheeps," she said. Cheap Cheeps was a discount store in Union Square that specialized in items for sale that every other retailer in the world turned down, things like discontinued, out-of-date, and just bad merchandise in general, all sold at rock-bottom prices. I'd shopped there a time or two myself, and if nothing else, it made for an entertaining experience.

"We'll check his office out. Thanks."

"Be careful when you talk to him," Tianna said. "I've heard that he has a temper."

Had they seriously not heard about what had happened in April Springs that morning? If not, I couldn't just leave them in the dark. "Someone attacked him at the ReNEWed building site last night," I told her loudly enough for the others to hear.

"Is he dead?" Tianna asked. "I didn't like the man, but I wouldn't wish that on him."

"No, he's still hanging in there, but it's still not sure whether he'll recover or not."

"Poor Jillian. She hasn't had much luck with the men in her life, and it appears that streak is still going strong. I need to call her," Tianna said. "Please be gentle with her, ladies. She's had a rough life."

"Will you give us half an hour before you talk to her?" I asked. I wanted to see how Jillian reacted to the news about what had happened to the contractor.

"I don't like keeping this from her, or you two ambushing her, either."

Evidently Angelica had been eavesdropping on our conversation, which was certainly her right since we were standing in her kitchen. "Tianna, trust Suzanne and Grace. You know they'll do the right thing."

The eldest daughter looked at her mother before nodding. "You have thirty minutes, starting now," she said firmly. "Remember to be nice to her."

"We'll do our best," I said.

As we drove to the tire center, I told Grace, "Is it just me, or does Masters seem to prey on damaged women?"

"Maybe Regina and Jillian, but that doesn't explain Gabby," she said.

"Maybe it was more of a financial thing with her," I said. "Besides, Gabby can be downright lovely when she puts her mind to it."

"True, but how often does she take the trouble to do that?" Grace asked with a grin.

I had to smile. "That's a fair point."

"Suzanne, the thing I'm trying to say is that maybe he thought of her as broken too because of her rough demeanor."

"It's entirely possible. This just keeps getting better and better, doesn't it?" I asked her.

"From what we've heard so far, it's amazing to me that no one attacked him *before* last night," Grace said, and then she immediately added, "I shouldn't have said that. After all, the poor man is in the hospital, and no one knows if he's even going to make it, and here I am taking potshots at him."

"It's okay," I said. "We're working hard to find who did this to him, so maybe we should get a little leeway in the way we talk about him, at least with each other."

"Good, because I despise *anyone* who preys on other people's weaknesses. They are the worst kind of bully as far as I'm concerned."

She'd said it with quite a bit of vehemence. "Did it feel good to get that out of your system?"

Grace shrugged. "You know me. I won't let my sense of outrage about his behavior slow my desire to figure out who did this. Even the creeps of the world deserve a little bit of my respect. Not a lot, but a little. That's all I'm saying."

Chapter 7

WE DIDN'T EVEN HAVE to ask Jillian her name, since it was emblazoned on her shirt at the tire store. They all wore the same outfits, whether they did the work in the garage or sold the tires or rang up the purchases. Jillian couldn't have been any more different from Regina at first glance. She sported mousy brown hair, wore makeup that was rather badly applied, and seemed to slouch all of the time. I doubted that she got much attention from the men around her, and I could see again how Mike Masters might have focused on her as prey. It amazed me how different Gabby was from the other two women we were dealing with, but I reminded myself that my friend had most likely been wooed for profit, while these young ladies had been pursued for sport. Either way, it didn't paint a very nice picture of the contractor, but I wasn't really doing this for him. Gabby was in trouble, and I would happily wade through the muck of Mike Masters's life to help her. To make matters worse, the closer I got to the young woman, the faster I realized that it appeared that Jillian had done a not-so-perfect job of trying to conceal a black eye.

"Jillian, do you have a second?" I asked her.

"I'm sorry, but if you want tires, you need to talk to Pete," she said as she gestured to a hearty man standing nearby dressed just like her.

"It's about Mike Masters," I said.

Her face went ashen. "What about him?" she asked. "Is he here?" she added as she looked quickly around the showroom. There was pure fright in her frantic gaze, and her entire body seemed to tense up at the mere mention of the man's name.

"He's in the hospital," Grace said. "Haven't you heard?"

"Nobody ever tells me anything," she answered in a defeated voice. "Did his heart finally explode on him?"

"Why do you ask that?" I wondered aloud.

"He was always saying that he wanted to live every bit of his life he could, and he didn't care what the consequences were. He was supposed to be taking medication for his high blood pressure, but he usually ignored it."

"This wasn't medical. Somebody attacked him at his worksite last night or early this morning," I said.

Jillian's eyes narrowed for a second as though she didn't believe me. "If you're kidding me, it's not very funny."

"I wish we were, but we're telling you the truth," Grace said. "When was the last time you saw him?"

"It was two nights ago," she said as she took it all in. "Pete, I'm taking my break."

"You've got ten minutes, Jillian, but that doesn't count if the truck comes in," he reminded her without even looking in her direction.

The three of us walked out the side door to a bench where it was clear the employees took their breaks. "Who did it? Who attacked him?" Jillian asked as she pulled out a pack of cigarettes and lit one. Just as quickly, she snuffed it out in the bucket of sand beside her that sported a dozen other butts. "I'm trying to quit," she said. "It's a bad habit."

"Like going out with guys like Mike Masters?" Grace asked her.

"I was giving him up, too," she said. "That was our last time together, no matter what."

"Was that your choice or his?" I asked her.

Jillian glared at me for an instant before catching herself. "I dumped him, no matter what he might have said afterwards." After a moment, she stared down at her hands before she spoke again. "How bad is it?"

"They don't know yet," I said. "He's still unconscious."

"You should talk to a woman named Regina. I don't know her last name, but she lives in April Springs. Either she did it or that old hag he was working for, Gabby Williams, did, but I guarantee you that it had something to do with his bad behavior. That's why I dumped him." That last addition was almost as though she'd just thought of it, and clearly she liked the way that it made her sound.

"Why do you say that?"

"The truth is that Mike wasn't exactly nice when it came to women," she said.

"Is that how you got the black eye?" I asked her gently.

"This? No, I ran into a door," she said woodenly, and it was clear that she was lying.

"We heard that he wasn't nice to his clients, either," Grace added.

"Yeah, I heard him bragging about that a few times. He called all of the people he worked for suckers," she admitted. "What did they use on him, a tire iron or something?"

"I heard that the police believe that it was a hammer from the construction site," I said.

"I guess that makes a crazy kind of sense," she said when Pete came out.

"Jillian, the truck's here. Every hand on deck. You know the drill."

"You help unload the tires here, too?" I asked her. She didn't look like she could lift all that much to me, and I had to wonder how she'd manage to wrestle those large tires.

"I'm pretty strong for my size," she said, bragging a bit as she did. "I can even outlift Pete," she added softly. "Sorry, but I've gotta go. It's too bad about Mike, but that part of my life is over once and for all. I'm sorry someone beat him up, but it's not my problem anymore."

We watched as Jillian walked around the building to where a semi had just pulled up with a load of tires in back.

"That was interesting," Grace said as she started to walk back to the Jeep. When she saw that I wasn't following, she turned back and asked me, "We're not going to wait for her to unload the truck, are we? We don't want to get Tianna angry with us, and besides, I have a feeling we got everything out of her that we're going to get without more leverage to use on her."

"So do I," I said, "but I want to see something."

Pete had jumped up into the back of the truck, and he handed a tire down to each employee in line. When it was Jillian's turn, she took the heavy tire as though it weighed next to nothing and walked it over to the stack with the best of them.

"She didn't lie about that," I said. "That girl is some kind of strong."

"So?"

"So it means that she could have held Mike up against that wall and nailed him to it after she knocked him out," I said. "Every person we've talked to seems to be physically capable of the act, even Gabby if she was angry enough."

"You're right," Grace said. "There's no doubt in my mind that Regina could do it. She looked as though she could hold her own in a tussle with a bear."

"Well, we're not going to learn anything new standing around here, so we might as well go," I told Grace.

"What's next on our agenda?" she asked me.

"I'd like to have a look at Mike's office. Even if we can't get inside, we can at least peek in through the windows," I said.

"Do you really think we'll find anything there?"

"I don't know, but we won't know until we check it out," I said with a shrug.

"Fine, but can we stop by Napoli's on the way back home after we do that?"

I looked at my best friend and grinned. "You're not hungry again already, are you?"

"Hey, a girl has to eat, doesn't she?" she asked me. "Are you saying you couldn't force yourself to take a bite or two of *anything* those ladies made?"

"After all these years, I'm not about to start lying to you now," I answered with a smile of my own. "But we need to go to Mike Masters's office first."

"That's fine by me. It's probably just a hole in the wall, anyway," Grace allowed. "Plus, we already know it's in a bad area of town. If the place is anywhere *near* Cheap Cheeps, it's going to be a dump."

"Maybe it will surprise us," I said.

It didn't.

There are nice strip malls that are well maintained and a pleasure to visit, but this wasn't one of them. The trim of the building needed a fresh coat of paint, and the parking lot looked as though it had been patched a dozen times over the years with varying degrees of success. A full third of the letters on the sign out front were missing, and it took me a few seconds to realize that AST had to be Mike Masters's office.

"Suite 206," Grace read off the board. "Does anything in this place look sweet to you?"

"That's the wrong kind of sweet, and you know it," I told her as we walked toward the office in question. The contractor's office was located between a sketchy-looking mail-order place and a bail bondsman's office.

As we approached the door, I saw that it was open.

Not only that, but it had clearly been kicked in.

I just hoped that whoever had done it was long gone, because one way or another, I was going to have my own look around that office.

Then I started having second thoughts. If the cops found us there, they might assume that we'd done it. It might be better to call them first and then have a look around while we waited for them.

Chapter 8

BEFORE I COULD TAKE out my cell phone though, Grace pushed the door the rest of the way open and stepped inside. The office had clearly been trashed by someone recently.

"What are you doing?" I asked her.

"I'm going to check out this office," she said. "How about you?"

"I was going to call the police first," I admitted.

"We can always do that *after* we look around," she said with the hint of a smile.

"What if a Union Square cop comes along before we can call this in? He might think that we did it ourselves," I answered.

"I'm sure we can talk our way out of that if it happens," she answered. "Come on."

I didn't put my phone away, but I didn't use it to dial 911, either. Instead, I started taking photos and video of the place. Maybe Grace was right. There was too much to take in before we had to call the police. The office, as small as it was, had been truly messed up. Every drawer of the desk had been pulled out, and the filing cabinet had been overturned, its contents spilled everywhere. I saw a hole in the wall where someone had punched his hand through it. "I'm guessing that whoever did this didn't find what they were looking for," I said as I took a picture of the hole.

"Do you think they punched the wall out of frustration?" she asked me.

"That would be my guess," I said. "What were they looking for?"

"I don't have a clue," Grace said as she took it all in. She knelt down to look at some of the papers lying in one of the piles, and I reached out a hand and stopped her.

"We don't want to leave any fingerprints," I reminded her, and she took a pen out of her purse and used that to move the papers around instead.

"These are all bills," she said.

"Did Masters really do that much work for people?" I asked as I looked around.

"They aren't that kind of bills. These aren't invoices for work he did; they are bills that he owed. No wonder he went after Jenny for that job. He was desperate for cash."

"Then I doubt anyone broke in here looking for money," I said. "One look in this office would tell anyone breaking in that they'd hit a dry hole."

"So maybe it wasn't money they were after," Grace said as the doorway darkened with someone's shadow.

"Can I help you with something, ladies?" a man's deep and gravelly voice asked behind us.

"We just got here," I explained before I noticed that the stranger wasn't wearing a uniform. He had the air of a cop about him though, and I had to wonder if he was plainclothes. "You're on the job, aren't you?" I asked, referring to law enforcement like Jake did sometimes to other cops.

"Used to be," he said. "You?"

"My husband, but he's retired," I added.

"Happens to the best of us." He took in the scene and then said, "I saw you drive up, so I know you didn't do this. I wish I could say I'm surprised, but that was the kind of clientele Masters brought in." He extended a meaty hand to me. "I'm Willis. I'm next door."

"The bail bondsman," I said, knowing for a fact that he didn't run that mail-order business.

"It's a living, though not by much." He took in the scene more fully. "I'd better call this in. Did you hear what happened to Masters?"

I nodded. "I'm the one who found him," I admitted.

Willis looked surprised. "That must have been a sight."

"I've seen worse," I admitted, which was certainly true. Grace stood there taking it all in, almost afraid to talk for fear of ruining our connection.

He just nodded. "Unless you two want to get dragged into this mess, I'd take off if I were you. Are you finished up here?"

"We are," I said as I stepped past him and out the door. "Thanks."

"You bet. Tell your husband that another old cop said hey."

"He'd want me to say hey right back," I said as I offered him a slight smile.

"Yeah, you're probably right about that," he answered with the hint of a grin of his own.

"What was that all about?" Grace asked as we got into the Jeep and drove away. It was all I could do not to speed, but I managed to keep my cool after all. "You were pretty cool in there, lady."

"I nearly swallowed my tongue when I thought we'd been caught by a cop," I admitted. "Once I knew he was retired, it was a piece of cake."

"You've got some serious game for a donutmaker," she answered. "So, what do you think the burglar was looking for in Masters's office?"

"I have no idea," I admitted. "I wouldn't think there would be *anything* worthwhile in there."

"It could have been a random act of violence," Grace offered.

"Neither one of us believe that," I answered. We got to the Napoli's parking lot, and I sat there a moment before getting out. "Are we sure we want to do this right now?"

"Why wouldn't we?" Grace asked.

"I don't know. I just feel as though we should be doing something else about the case."

"Suzanne, I'm not quite sure what else we *can* do at the moment," Grace admitted. "We've talked to all of the suspects we've been able to find, and until something else turns up, I'm at a loss as to what to do next, at least for the time being."

"I guess you're right, but I can't help thinking that we've missed something along the way."

"Don't worry. If we have, it will come to us," Grace said. "In the meantime, let's go get something amazing to eat and visit a bit with our friends again."

"How was Jillian?" Tianna asked us the second we walked back into the kitchen at Napoli's. "I called her, but she didn't pick up."

"Not great," I admitted. "She tried to hide it with makeup, but she had a black eye."

Tianna bristled. "That jerk! Why was she even dating him after that happened?"

"She told us that she dumped him, if that means anything," I said softly. "She's giving up smoking, too. From the looks of it, she's really trying to get her life on track."

"I'll try calling her again," Tianna said. "Thanks for taking it easy on her."

Grace added, "Don't worry. We had to press her a little, but we were gentle about it."

"I know you can't dance around some things," Tianna said. "Sometimes you don't have any choice but to ask the hard questions."

"What are you three whispering about?" Angelica asked us as she approached. She'd been busy filling orders when we'd come in, and only after doing that did she have time to spare for us. It honored me that she treated us like family and felt free to ignore us if she was busy.

"We were talking about Jillian," Tianna told her mother.

"How is she?" Angelica asked as she looked at us.

"On the mend," I said, and I meant it.

"That's a good thing, then. Now, what can I feed you both? I should warn you that neither one of you is leaving here without a full belly and a big smile." She wasn't even grinning as she said it, and I knew that she meant business.

Inspiration suddenly struck. "Could you make us up a meal for four to-go?" I asked.

Grace nodded in approval. "We want to surprise our guys with dinner," she added.

"I'd be delighted," Angelica said.

"Let's see, for starters we'll have..." I started to say before I was interrupted.

"If you don't mind, I'll handle the menu myself, from appetizers all the way through the desserts."

"Why would I mind you doing that?" I asked her.

"Excellent," she said.

"By the way, what are we having?" I asked her.

"You'll find out when you open the bags, but don't do it until you get home. It's a surprise," she said.

"Hey, I like surprises," I answered.

"How much do I owe you?" I asked Angelica as she started putting together a pair of large bags filled with food. I couldn't imagine what she was going to charge me, but whatever it was would surely be worth it. I watched her add figures on a calculator and even consult Sophia at one point. Once Angelica was satisfied with the total, she walked over to me with a frown on her face. "It's close to sixty dollars, but I honestly don't like charging you."

"Sometimes we don't always get what we want," I told her with a smile as I handed her three twenties.

"Fine, you win," Angelica said. "Oh, one second. I forgot something." She turned her back and soon returned with our bags of food. "Your change is in the bag."

Tianna said, "Mom, there's a party at table 14 that wants to talk to you."

"Why? Is there a problem?" she asked.

"No, they want to compliment the chef," she said with a smile.

Sophia took off her apron and handed it to her sister. "Then why are you telling *her*? After all, I'm the one who made all of the food today."

Tianna protested. "Sophia, that's not the way we do things here, and you know it."

"I was just teasing," Sophia said as she reached for her apron again. Angelica wouldn't allow it, though. "No, you're right. You *should* go."

"Mom, it was a joke."

"Go on, Sophia. They are waiting for you," Angelica said stoically.

"Then we'll *both* go," Sophia said as she put her arm in her mother's. "They're in luck, because they get two chefs for the price of one today."

Angelica allowed her youngest to pull her out into the dining area, and Tianna turned to us before we left and nodded. I hoped that her friend, Jillian, gave us a good report when they spoke.

As Grace and I walked out to the Jeep, she asked, "I wonder what we're having?"

"I don't know, but you heard Angelica. There's no peeking. We'll see it when the guys do," I said as I stowed my bag in back and made room for her to put hers down as well. "Do you think there's a chance Jake and Stephen will carve out some time to join us?"

"They will when they find out where this food came from," Grace said. "Let's give them a call at the same time."

I agreed, and before we left the back parking area, I pulled out my cell phone and called Jake. "How would you like a catered meal for four from Napoli's for dinner tonight? We've got enough for Grace and Stephen to share with us, too."

"Suzanne, I was just about to call you," he said soberly. "Mike Masters died twenty minutes ago."

Chapter 9

"DID HE EVER EVEN WAKE up?" I asked as I heard Grace get the same news from Chief Grant.

"No, he never did," Jake said.

"I suppose that means that dinner is off," I answered.

"I don't see why it has to be. There's nothing we have to do now that we weren't already doing. I could use a break, but I don't know about the chief."

"Grace is asking him right now," I said.

"He said dinner is fine. We're eating at my place. Is that okay?" she asked after she hung up. "At least that's what I told Stephen."

"That would be great," I said, and then I turned back to my phone. "We're all eating at Grace's house. We'll be there in half an hour."

"We'll meet you there," Jake said.

Our drive home was quite a bit more somber than it would have been had we not just gotten the bad news. I certainly hadn't been a fan of Mike Masters in any way, shape, or form, but that didn't mean that his death didn't sadden me. If he'd been given the time, maybe he could have turned over a new leaf like Jillian was trying to do, but now he'd never get the opportunity to correct his past sins.

Grace and I were fully in it now.

What had started as an assault case was now flat-out murder, and the pressure to find the killer had just intensified one thousand percent.

"Who do you think did it?" Grace asked me halfway through the drive home.

"I don't know," I admitted. "I can start by saying that I don't think there's a chance in the world that Gabby did it. Can you see her actually doing something like that?"

"She might hit him, but she wouldn't nail him to the wall," Grace said with a shrug. "That takes a special kind of hate to do something like that."

"Sure, but she was nursing two pretty recent wounds, one financial and the other one romantic," I said.

"Would she even know how to operate a nail gun?" she asked me.

"I don't know, but maybe we should find out," I said.

"Suzanne, you don't think she attacked him, do you? Are you having second thoughts?" Grace asked me.

"No, but then again, I can't imagine *anyone* in their right mind doing it either, so we should at least have another chat with Gabby the next time we see her," I admitted. "Jillian could have done it after getting a black eye. Regina certainly had the strength to as well."

"Is there anybody else we need to consider?"

"Not that we've found yet," I said, "but he wasn't working that job alone. How about his crew? One of them could have done it."

"That's a good idea. We need to check that out in the morning," Grace said. "Do you think his crew will show up for work tomorrow after the crime scene's been cleared?"

"I doubt it. We're probably going to have to track them down," I answered.

"That's okay. We can do that, too," Grace said.

Jake and Chief Grant were waiting on us when we pulled into Grace's driveway, and they offered to grab the bags as we walked inside to set the table.

"Wow, what brought this on?" Stephen asked us after he kissed Grace.

"We thought you both might like a break," I said.

"You thought right," Jake answered as I got a kiss of my own. "There's just one ground rule, if you ladies agree."

"You two are not getting more of this food than we are," I said.

Jake looked surprised. "Do you honestly think we'd ever suggest that? I feel fortunate that you didn't stop halfway here and start eating."

"How do you know we didn't?" I asked him with a laugh.

"What's the rule?" Grace wanted to know.

"Let's not talk about Mike Masters, at least during the meal," Stephen said. "It's just too much to deal with at the moment, and I'm sure we could all use a break from the case."

"Agreed," I said promptly.

"Of course," Grace added. "Come on and eat."

"What do we have?" the police chief asked, and for a moment he looked his age, which was younger than any of the rest of us.

"We have no idea," I said. "That was the bargain I made with Angelica."

"What deal is that?" Jake asked me.

"I demanded that she let us pay for the meal, but she wasn't happy about it," I said as we walked into Grace's house.

As she and Stephen set the dining room table, Jake and I opened the spread to see just what we'd be dining on.

"Hey, there's money in this one," Jake said.

"She told me she dropped the change in the bag," I explained.

Jake held up my original three twenties and grinned. "If this is the change, how much did you give her?"

"Blast it, she tricked me," I said, unhappy with this turn of events. I thought she had agreed to letting me pay too easily. I reached for my phone before Jake stopped me.

"What are you doing, Suzanne?"

"I'm going to talk to Angelica and straighten this out once and for all," I said.

"Maybe you'd better wait until you can do it calmly," Jake suggested softly.

"I'm calm!" I shouted without realizing that was what I'd done. "Maybe you're right. Things can't keep on like this, though."

"So you'll straighten it out the next time you see her," he said. "In the meantime, we still need to eat, and I'm not about to waste this food over a principle."

"I guess you're right," I reluctantly agreed.

"It happens sometimes," he said with a soft smile. "What do you have in that bag?"

"This one's chicken Kiev," I said as I opened the container.

"Ooh, I want that," Grace answered as she reached for it.

"I've got lasagna," Jake said.

"Okay, I want that, too," she answered.

"Are you going to actually let the rest of us eat, too?" Stephen asked her.

"Of course I am," Grace replied with a smile. "After Suzanne and I fill our plates, you two are more than welcome to argue over the scraps that are left behind."

Jake grinned at the chief. "Don't sweat it, Stephen. Angelica packed enough food to feed an army. She sent ravioli, too?"

"I don't know about the rest of you, but I'm starting with that," I said.

As Jake had predicted, there was enough food to feed three times as many people even after we were finished. "Does anyone have room for dessert?" I asked as I started clearing away the plates.

"I'm too stuffed to move," Chief Grant said. "How about you, Jake?"

"It depends," he said. "What do we have?"

"You are not getting any," I told him.

"Not even a sliver? I don't need much, just a taste," he protested meekly.

"Okay, maybe a little bit," I said with a grin. "I might even join you," I added as I spooned out some tiramisu.

"That looks good," Chief Grant said as he watched our plates receive healthy portions.

"There are some cannolis, too," I replied.

"I could handle a few of those," he admitted with a grin.

"Grace? How about you?" I asked her.

"I'm good for now," she said. "Does anyone want coffee?"

"That would be perfect," Jake answered. "How long do we have until we need to get back, Chief?" he deferred to his volunteer boss.

"Fifteen, twenty minutes? How does that sound?"

"It works for me," Jake said.

I was about to ask him what they were going to do next when I remembered the rule the men had proposed. While technically dinner was over, I wasn't in the mood to ruin our fun time. I considered asking Stephen and Grace if they'd set a wedding date yet, but that might put a damper on things, too. What was there safe to talk about? I was still trying to come up with a topic when Chief Grant, of all people, spoke up for me. "Grace and I are thinking about going overseas for a little vacation," he said.

She looked at him and smiled. "I didn't think you were going to tell them just yet."

"What can I say? I'm a man of whimsy and impulse."

We all had to laugh at that. When he'd been a regular cop, Stephen Grant had been a man full of laughter and lightness, but since taking over the chief of police position, he'd developed a much more somber side I'd never seen coming.

"Hey, I'm a fun guy," he protested.

I grinned. "Sure you are."

"Before anybody asks, we're not talking about a honeymoon," Grace said with a smile. "We're not sure when we're going to get married, but that doesn't mean that we can't take a trip together before that happens." Her grin broadened as she added, "You know what? You two should go with us."

"Really? Is that okay with you, Stephen?" I asked him.

"I think it's a great idea," he answered. "I'm just sorry that I didn't think of it myself."

"Where were you thinking about going?" Jake asked him.

"That's the rub. Maybe you can help us decide."

"I've got an idea," I said. "Grace, I need four pens and some paper."

"Okay, what's your idea first?"

"We each write down where we'd like to go, and then someone reads them aloud. That way nobody will cheat," I said as I looked at her.

"I *never* cheat," she said as she smiled. "I just stack the odds in my favor sometimes."

"How is that *not* cheating?" Jake asked good-naturedly.

"It's all in how you look at it. Come on, this sounds like fun."

We each wrote down our choices and put them in one of Grace's floppy hats. As she pulled out the names, showing us all before dropping each one onto the table, I wrote them down.

SCOTLAND

DUBLIN

PARIS

VIRGIN ISLANDS

"Leave it to the four of us to come up with four different countries," I said. "I've got a feeling we'll never be able to agree. Who chose what?" I knew two of the answers, but Grace and Stephen might not.

"Scotland's mine," Jake admitted.

"I put Paris in the hat," I said. "We had such a lovely time on our honeymoon that I've been dying to go back ever since."

"I picked the Virgin Islands," Stephen Grant said, surprising me.

"Seriously?"

"I'd love some sand, some sun, and some crystal-clear water," he admitted.

"You picked Dublin?" I asked Grace. How had she still managed to surprise me even after all of these years?

"I saw a show the other night about their brightly colored doors, and I've been dying to see them for myself ever since," she admitted.

"What should we do, folks?" I asked them. "Does anyone have *any* ideas that might work?"

"We could throw caution to the wind," Chief Grant said with a huge grin. "You three don't think I can be spontaneous? I'll show you. Put the names back into the hat, Suzanne. Whichever place you draw first is where we go."

"I love it," I said. "Jake?"

"They all work for me," he said after a moment's thought.

"Grace?"

"You know me. I was a born gambler. Let's roll the dice."

"Okay, but I'm not picking the winner," I said.

Grace grabbed the hat. "I'll do it."

She reached in, and with great fanfare withdrew a name.

"Scotland it is," she said. "Ooh, castles and cool landscapes would be awesome."

"Not to mention the whiskey," Jake said.

"Is *that* the reason you put that name in the hat?" I asked him.

"No, I want to see the castles and landscapes, too, but I'd be lying if I said I didn't want to do it with a glass in my hands."

"Then it's settled," Chief Grant said. "Before we let too much time pass, we're all going on vacation together to Scotland. Life is too short not to enjoy every bit of it while we can."

It was a fun idea, and a somber thought, to end our dinner party on, but somehow it was appropriate. I was already looking forward to the trip, and it had just come up not even half an hour before. Good ideas were like that sometimes. I had a tendency to overthink everything, and with this crowd, I'd never get the chance. It sounded as though it would be the perfect amount of mayhem I needed in my life. We could swing it financially too, if we didn't stay in the very best accommodations and we flew as cheaply as we could. If we had to dig into our hard-earned savings to make it happen, I was willing to do it.

After all, trips like this one promised to be were too special to let a little money stand in the way.

We'd eat peanut butter and jelly sandwiches for a year if we had to in order to make this trip work, and what was more, we'd do it with broad smiles.

Chapter 10

"WHAT ARE YOU GOING to do now that Jake and Stephen have gone back to the office?" I asked Grace after we finished cleaning up. I'd been right. There had been enough leftovers for all four of us to have another meal. The next time I went to Napoli's, I was going to take four dozen donuts with me, and I felt sorry for Angelica if she tried to pay me for them. After that, we were going to have a little chat about money and the value of friendship.

"I hate to be a party pooper, but I could use the time to do some work," she said. "If we're going to keep digging into what has turned out to be murder, I need to get some things taken care of first."

"I can take a hint," I said as I hugged her. "I'll see you tomorrow after the donut shop closes."

"I'll be there with bells on," she said. "It's good to be back."

"I didn't know you ever left," I told her as I gathered up our share of the food.

"You know what I mean. I missed investigating cases with you," Grace answered.

"Why wouldn't you? I'm fun to hang around with, especially if you don't count the times I manage to put our lives in jeopardy."

"And yet we still somehow manage to come out all right on the other end," Grace said as she walked me to her door.

"So far, anyway."

I drove my Jeep back home, a journey of less than a hundred yards, and once I was back at the cottage, I put our share of the leftovers in the fridge. I knew what Jake and I would be eating sometime in the next few days, and I was already getting excited about it.

After that was accomplished, I sat on the couch and tried to watch an old movie, but I kept losing interest. It wasn't the movie's fault. Evidently I just wasn't in the mood to sit still. I decided to take a walk through the park to see if I could clear my head, so after locking up, I took a nice stroll out my front door. It was downright handy having a park so close to the cottage, and I knew that I didn't take advantage of it nearly enough.

There weren't many folks out despite how lovely the evening was, so I mostly had the park to myself except for a pair of teenagers trying to find a quiet place to hang out and just be together. I did my best not to make eye contact with them, especially since I knew the girl—as well as her mother—pretty well. She'd first come to my donut shop as a grade schooler, and here she was out with a boy.

It suddenly made me feel old.

I decided to walk over to Donut Hearts and have a look around while I was out and about. After all, it was a point of pride for me that I owned the place, and I reveled in it when I could take the time to actually stop and enjoy the feeling.

As I neared my shop's front door, I looked around and spotted a beat-up, crusty old white van parked down the street. It didn't have any markings on it, but it had clearly led a hard life. I was sure the paint had once been bright white, but it had faded quite a bit in the years since. Two men were sitting in the front seat, and when they noticed that I was looking at them, the driver started the vehicle and drove away a little faster than he should have on Springs Drive. I took out my phone to get a photo of the license plate, but gobs of mud obscured the numbers. Had that been a part of the general neglected state of the van, or had it been done deliberately? "Suzanne, you're getting paranoid even for you," I said to myself softly.

And then I heard a sound coming from ReNEWed. There was police tape still up warning folks not to cross over, but evidently someone had decided to ignore that particular rule, and I was going to see if I could find out who it was. I figured I could walk around the building and peek inside without putting myself in any real jeopardy. After all,

I could always just run back home if I found out that I was about to wrangle with a real bad guy.

At least that was what I told myself as I explored a little further.

"Gabby, you shouldn't be in there," I said as I looked in through one of the windows. More accurately, it was a place where a window would someday be. At the moment, it was just a framed opening, and unlike the front, the plastic that had covered it at one point had been completely cut away.

"It's *my* shop, Suzanne," she said, clearly unhappy about being caught there. "What are you doing lurking around in the bushes?"

"There aren't any bushes out here," I argued.

"I was speaking metaphorically," she answered. "You know what I mean."

"I heard a noise, and I wanted to see what was going on. I thought somebody might be vandalizing the place."

She softened at that. "I appreciate you looking out for my best interests, but there's no need for you to be here."

"Since I'm looking out for your interests anyway, you shouldn't be in there, Gabby. That police tape is there for a reason."

"Are you telling me that you've never ignored a warning like that yourself?" she asked me pointedly.

"We're not talking about me," I said. "What are you doing in there?"

"Honestly, I'm trying to figure out what to do with this place," she said.

"You're not thinking about giving up, are you?" I had grown used to the idea of having Gabby nearby again, and the prospect of her abandoning her shop, and me, wasn't something I wanted to face. Whether I liked it or not, our friendship had become important to me, and I didn't want to see it disappear, especially given the circumstances.

"A man was murdered here," Gabby said. "How am I *not* going to see Mike's body every time I walk through that front door?"

She should talk. I had been the one to find Mike Masters pinned to the wall like a science exhibit, and though he'd still been alive when I'd first found him, that was no longer the case. "If I can get past it, then so should you," I told her. "You can't let one bad thing outweigh all of the good ones."

"I know you've had more than your share of trouble and tragedy at the donut shop, and for the life of me, I don't see how you still come to work every day."

"You have to take the good with the bad in this world, Gabby."

"Maybe you do. I'm not sure that I do."

She started to move toward the door opening in the rear, and I could see that the plastic had been removed there as well. The warning tape was still intact though, and Gabby stepped deftly over it. Had she moved it down to make it easier to walk over, or had it been installed that way? If I had to guess, I'd say that Gabby had done it to make things easier on herself.

Once she was back outside of the cordoned-off perimeter, she asked, "Have you made any progress yet? Things have suddenly gotten uglier now."

"We just got started," I reminded her.

"I know that, but surely you've come up with *something*. You've had hours."

I wasn't in the mood to be scolded, but I wasn't sure that was the time or the place to protest. "We've found some people who knew Mike fairly well," I said as delicately as I could.

"Women," she said. "You found the tramp in Union Square, didn't you?"

It was hard to think of Jillian Christie as a tramp. "It wasn't like that, Gabby," I said.

"Are you seriously defending this woman?" she asked. There was no doubt that Gabby was legitimately furious with me at that moment, and I saw a hot temper that went beyond anything I'd ever seen in her before.

"He tricked you!" I said, slapping her with the words. "What makes you think he didn't fool the other women in his life, too? All three of you were victims as far as I'm concerned."

That got her attention. "I never thought about it that way, but you're absolutely right. I'm sorry I blew up. Who are they? I have a right to know, Suzanne."

I wasn't sure that was true, especially given the temper flare-up I'd just witnessed. "I don't want you talking to either one of them, Gabby."

"I wouldn't do that," she said, though she averted her eyes as she did.

"Do I have your word on that?" I asked her. "I'm serious here. Don't give it if you're not willing to back it up. Our friendship depends on it."

She started to speak, then waited a few moments, clearly giving my threat more consideration. After a few more heartbeats, she said, "I promise."

"No contact of any kind," I repeated.

"I get it."

From the look in her eyes, I could see that she meant it, and what was more, she knew that I was dead serious, too. I was still taking a chance sharing my information with her, but if I couldn't trust her to live up to her word, then we were finished anyway. "Apparently Mike was seeing a woman named Jillian Christie in Union Square. I spoke with her, and she told me that *she* broke up with *him*. *She* ended it, Gabby."

"Did you believe her?"

"It's a little more complicated than that," I said. While it was true that I wanted to believe Jillian, that black eye had troubled me, and with Mike Masters dead, there was no one to dispute her side of what had happened between them.

"What about the other one?"

This would be a little stickier. "Remember what you told me."

"I'm not about to risk losing one of my best friends over this," she said, a touching sentiment to say the least.

"He had something casual going on with Regina Davis," I said. "Do you know her?"

"Oh, yes," she said. "Was *that* the kind of woman he really wanted? It feels as though I didn't even know the man."

"I'm sorry," was all that I could think to say.

"It's not your fault, Suzanne," she said as she smiled softly at me. "Do you think either one of them did it?"

"All I can say is that they're both still on our suspect list," I said.

"Our? I thought Jake was working with Chief Grant."

"He is. Grace is helping me," I said.

"Good. I don't want you to take any chances, even if it's for me. I couldn't live with myself if something happened to one of you."

That was the Gabby I saw glimpses of from time to time, the soft and kind woman I was proud to think of as my friend. If only she'd let that side show to the world more.

"We'll be careful," I said. "In the meantime, you shouldn't be here. Why don't you go home and try not to think about what happened?"

"If I could figure out a way to do that, I'd be amazed, but I suppose the least I can do is try."

"Would you like me to walk you home?" I offered. "We can even go get the Jeep so I can drive you."

"No, I need some time to think, and I believe a walk is just what I need at the moment. You don't mind if I go on alone, do you?"

"Of course not. I understand completely." I tried to offer what comfort I could, but it wasn't much, and I knew it. "It'll all turn out in the end, Gabby."

"Isn't that just wishful thinking on your part?" she asked me as she started to walk away.

"What can I say? I try to be positive when I can," I told her.

"Then you're a better woman than I am. Good night, Suzanne."

"Good night, Gabby."

I stood there and watched her walk down Springs Drive, her head held low and her posture, usually perfect, slumped from the weight of the world that was now on her shoulders. If I could do anything to alleviate that, I would, but for the moment, I needed to get back to the cottage and get some sleep before it was time to make the donuts yet again.

Unfortunately, that was not to be.

At least not right away.

Chapter 11

"I KNOW YOU'RE IN THERE, Suzanne!" Ray Blake, the newspaper owner, called out as he pounded on my front door. "I see your Jeep, and I know for a fact that Jake is working with the chief. Are you seriously ducking me?"

He continued to bang on my front door, something that I was sure was worse for his hand than it was for my entry.

"What's your problem, Ray?" I asked from four steps behind him.

Up until that moment, I always thought that saying someone jumped out of their skin was just a metaphor, but that was nearly what Ray did when he heard my voice from behind him.

"Suzanne, what are you doing sneaking up on me?" he asked as he whirled around, clearly embarrassed by his reaction to my approach.

"How can I be sneaking up on you if I'm walking up to my own cottage's front door?" I asked him. "What's so urgent, Ray?"

"I need your reaction to Mike Masters's murder for the paper," he said. "I only have twenty minutes before I have to go to press."

"I'm sorry, but you're doing it again," I told him with a frown.

"Doing what?"

"Mistaking your priorities and needs for mine," I said.

"You're not going to give me *anything*?" he asked incredulously.

"Sorry, but I don't have anything *for* you. Now if you'll excuse me, I'd like to go inside and get ready for bed. Your daughter and I are making donuts together in the morning, and I know you don't want me to have to tell her you kept me up past my bedtime."

"No, I absolutely don't want that," he admitted.

Even mentioning Emma was bringing out the big guns when it came to Ray. If I really wanted to shake him up, all I had to do was mention Sharon, his wife. For the longest time, I'd had trouble remembering the poor woman's name even though I'd known her forever, but once she started helping Emma at the donut shop on my days off, I knew that I'd never forget it again.

"But why won't you at least give me a quote?"

"Mainly because I have no desire to see my name in your newspaper ever again," I admitted. Ray had mentioned me more than enough in the past, always in reference to a case I was working on or had just solved, and if I never got my name in print again, that would be just fine with me.

"What if I quote you as an unnamed source?" he offered.

"Everybody who is going to read your paper knows that I'm the one who found Mike," I reminded him. "How much anonymity do you think that gives me?"

"You're right. I'm sorry I bothered you," Ray said as he headed for his car.

I felt bad about not helping him, and I wondered if there was anything I could give him that wouldn't be directly attributed to me, but for the life of me, I couldn't come up with a single thing. "Good luck with the story."

"Thanks," he said, not even looking back at me. I'd have to find a way to make it up to him, but for the moment, there was nothing I could really do.

And then it hit me. I might be able to help the newspaperman out and my friend Gabby at the same time. "Ray, hang on a second."

"What is it, Suzanne? I already apologized. What more do you want from me?"

"Are you by any chance slanting your article to make Gabby Williams look guilty?"

The expression on his face was enough to tell me that I'd hit home with my first shot. "I'm not really at liberty to discuss that."

"What if I told you that there were at least two other women Mike Masters was seeing at the time of his death and that they are both persons of interest in the investigation?"

"The police chief will confirm that?" he asked me hopefully.

"I didn't claim that it was an *official* investigation," I told him.

"What are their names?" he asked me, his handheld recorder held out toward me.

"I'm not giving those to you, and you know it, but I spoke with both women today personally, and I can guarantee you that they each have pretty powerful motives to want to see harm come to Mike Masters." I felt bad about throwing Jillian and Regina under the bus, but Gabby was my main priority.

"If it's not an official investigation, everyone is going to know it's coming from you no matter how I word it," he said with a frown.

"Come on, Ray, I've read your newspaper before, remember? You can find a way around that, and we both know it," I told him. "If you can't make folks wonder who you got the information from, then I think you might be losing your touch."

"You and I both know that I still have it," he said defiantly.

"We do. Just make sure it doesn't come back to bite me," I told him. "I'm doing this to help you out, Ray, so don't forget it."

"It also happens to help your friend, Gabby, at the same time too though, doesn't it?"

Maybe Ray wasn't as obtuse as I'd thought. "So what if it does? Are you accusing me of lying to you in order to protect her?"

"No, of course not," Ray said quickly. He instantly realized that he was on dangerous ground. I knew it too, but then again, I'd pushed him there myself. "You have my word. I'll do my best to make certain that no one will suspect that you are my source."

"You'd better, because if anybody asks, I'm going to deny we even spoke," I told him.

"I won't blame you if you do," he answered.

"Good. Then as long as we understand each other, I'll say good night."

"Good night, Suzanne, and thanks."

"For what? We never spoke, remember?"

Ray shook his head as he smiled. "Maybe I'm getting old after all. I don't know what I was thinking."

As he drove away, I wondered if I'd done the right thing. I hadn't even talked to Jake and Chief Grant about the two other women in the contractor's life yet, and I'd just acknowledged their existence to the nosiest man in four counties.

I understood that I had done what I had to do, but that didn't mean that I was all that happy about it.

"Hey, Jake, I need to talk to you. Do you have a second?" I asked him after I got him on the line.

"You're in luck, because I can give you a full minute," Jake said, laughing softly. "What's up?"

"I just did something that might backfire on me, and I wanted to let you know about it first," I admitted.

"Are you in any danger?" he asked me curtly. Suddenly there wasn't a hint of playfulness in his voice.

"No, not physically, at least. Ray Blake just left our cottage, and I told him in no uncertain words that there were two other women Mike had been seeing lately." Telling my husband made me feel better. Just getting it off my chest was helpful, but I braced myself for his reaction.

"Did you give him their names?" he asked.

"No, I didn't even tell him where they were from," I admitted.

"Suzanne, it's common knowledge that Mike Masters was the worst kind of tomcat. I'm guessing that you and Grace spoke with these women today. Am I right?"

"You haven't had us followed, have you?" I asked him, wondering how else he would know.

"Of course not. I just know the way your mind works. Let me guess. You turned up Regina Davis and Jillian Christie. Am I right?"

"You're dead on the money on both of them," I said. "How did you know?"

"You and Grace aren't the only ones good at investigating," he said. "Did you tell him anything else?"

"Just that if he attributed anything to me, I'd sic his wife and his daughter on him," I told him.

That made Jake chuckle again. "Then you should be fine. Was there anything else?"

"Just that I love you," I told him.

"Right back at you," he said before hanging up.

At least I'd be able to go to sleep with a relatively clear conscience now. They say that confession is good for the soul, and as far as keeping information from my husband was concerned, I would have to wholeheartedly agree. I'd been burned in marriage before by secrets, and I'd vowed never to allow them into a marriage again, and so far, I'd been able to do just that.

I felt Jake settle in beside me late that night. "Everything okay?" I asked groggily.

"It's fine. Go back to sleep," he said as he kissed my forehead.

I did just that, sleeping better now that he was beside me.

As was my usual custom, I woke up two minutes before my alarm went off. I wasn't even sure why I bothered setting it, but I knew if I didn't, that would be the morning my internal alarm failed to wake me up.

I got dressed silently and grabbed a quick bit of cereal before leaving the cottage. Before I walked out the door though, I went back into our bedroom and kissed Jake good-bye. It wasn't my normal habit, but then again, we weren't usually both trying to track a killer down. If something happened to either one of us, which I hoped with all of my heart that it didn't, I wanted our last memories of each other to be of love and of caring and of tenderness.

"Happy hunting today," I whispered to him.

"You, too," he answered, though I couldn't swear that he was completely awake as he said it.

I was surprised to see a light on at Donut Hearts as I drove up to the shop. Had I left one on the day before, or was there a more ominous reason for it?

I was about to call 911 when I spotted Emma in the front, waving to me and smiling. After I put my phone away, I got out of the Jeep and walked in.

"Did I miss something? I'm supposed to be here today, right?" I asked her as I took off my windbreaker.

"That's what the schedule says," she answered.

"So you're not due until four," I said.

"What can I say? I couldn't sleep. Some hotshot from Atlanta is trying to buy Barton and make him move down there to run his restaurants."

Barton Gleason was Emma's wildly talented chef/boyfriend, and the only thing that surprised me about her statement was that it hadn't happened sooner. I had a feeling that if Emma hadn't been in the picture, he would have been perfectly happy to move, but I had to give the young man credit. He knew a good woman when he found her, and he wasn't about to let her go.

"He's not going to take the offer, is he?"

"He says he's happy running his own place, but how can he be?" she asked. "We both know that he's destined for greater things. We spent all night discussing the possibilities, but in the end he decided to turn it down."

"Did he ask you to go with him again?" I asked.

"He said that he knew I wasn't ready, and he respected that. Honestly, I'm not sure why he hangs around."

I hugged her. "I've got a pretty good guess."

She blushed a bit. "Anyway, I thought you and I could work together making the cake donuts this morning. What do you think?"

"I think that sounds like fun," I said. "Tell you what. Let's try something completely different."

That was in Emma's wheelhouse. She loved experimenting with our coffee choices, and on her days of running the shop, I knew that she sometimes offered off-the-menu items that I'd never even dreamed about. "You know I'm always up for it," she said.

"Do you have any thoughts in particular?"

"How about a peach-and-raspberry cake donut with a vanilla bean frosting?" she asked.

"I'm game if you are, but I don't think we have either one of those fruits in our stock."

Emma grinned at me. "I bought some yesterday thinking that it might be fun to try," she admitted. "I have enough in back to make a dozen. What do you say?"

"Let's do it."

As I prepared the basic cake donut batter we used for all of our first run of donuts, Emma got the peaches and raspberries and made a chunky puree with them. I separated the master recipe into half a dozen different smaller bowls and slid one across the counter to Emma. As I mixed up our standard cake offerings, Emma worked on hers, and soon enough, we were ready to load up the dropper with our different batters and start frying. I worked my way through mine, rinsing the dropper in between batters, and after I was finished, I handed the tool to Emma. "I don't know how those are going to taste, but they smell wonderful," I told her.

"I know, right?" she asked with a grin.

"While you're doing that, I'll mix up some special icing," I said. I took some confectioners' sugar, a little water, and some pure vanilla paste we saved for special occasions, then I mixed up a slurry glaze. As each of her batches came out of the fryer, Emma put them on a different rack with a cookie sheet under it so I could apply the glaze by hand to each one.

We didn't even wait for the last batch to finish before we split a donut and tasted it.

"It's a little unimpressive, isn't it?" Emma asked. "I don't think I used enough peaches."

"Any more and it would have been too watered down. I'm not so sure they aren't too watery as they are right now. Maybe some extract instead of the real thing?"

"Do they even make peach extract?" she asked me.

"Absolutely. Let's try these again after we get a bottle. We can add the peach puree to the icing instead of the batter," I told her. "In the meantime, they're still pretty good."

"But they'd be even better with a light apricot glaze," she said. "Don't glaze the last batch, and I'll whip something up."

We had a hot plate in back that we rarely used, and Emma pulled an old bottle of apricot jam out of the fridge and put it into a saucepan. The timer went off, and I retrieved the donuts from the oil as she heated the jam. It hadn't had a chance to reduce much, but she still drizzled a bit on top of one of the donuts. We again tasted it, and the results this time were quite a bit better. "I'm going to glaze the rest of the dozen," she said.

"Even with the vanilla glaze already on them?"

"Why not? The worst thing that could happen is that we'd have to throw them out," Emma said. She did exactly as she'd said, tasted a bite of one, and then handed the rest to me. "What do you think, Suzanne?"

"Is it good or bad?" I asked before I took it from her.

"I'll let you be the judge of that," she replied.

I tasted it and was pleasantly surprised how well the flavor combination worked. "These are good enough to sell as is," I said.

"Let's put them out and see if anybody bites, then," she answered. "That was fun."

"Agreed," I said. "Let me mix up the dough for the raised donuts, and we can take our break."

"I can never get over the fact that it seems a lot longer when you start at the beginning," Emma said as she started washing up.

"It's funny how that works out, isn't it?" I asked her with a grin.

By the time I got the yeast dough ready for its first rising, Emma had made a real dent in the dirty dishes.

"Are you ready for our break?" I asked her as I set the timer.

"Honestly, I should probably finish these up first," she answered.

"They'll wait," I said as I headed for the kitchen door. "Come on. We can split another peach-and-raspberry donut."

"I want my own," she said with a smile. "At this rate, we won't have any to sell at all."

"I've been thinking about it, and I don't think we should," I told her.

"Did you change your mind? I thought you liked them."

"I do. That's why I'd like to do something I've been thinking about trying for a few weeks. Let's cut the donuts up into small samples as folks come in and offer them for free. Once they've tasted them, we can keep a tally of who thinks they might be a nice addition to the menu, or if they need more work. It might be a way to make everyone feel more invested in what we offer."

"That's brilliant, Suzanne. You're always thinking about Donut Hearts, aren't you?" she asked me as we grabbed donuts and coffee and walked outside.

"It's kind of what I do," I said as I glanced over at ReNEWed. It looked eerily quiet over there, and I wondered if anyone would ever finish it, or if I'd just be staring at an empty, unfinished shell for the rest of my life.

Emma must have caught my glance. "I can't believe someone attacked Mike Masters there. I hope he pulls through."

"Haven't you heard?" I asked her.

"Heard what? I was at Barton's late, and by the time I got home, Mom and Dad were already in bed. What about him?"

"Emma, I hate to be the one to tell you this, but Mike Masters is dead."

Chapter 12

"WHAT DO YOU MEAN HE'S dead?" she asked me as she slumped down in the outside chair.

"I just assumed that you knew," I said. "I'm sorry that you had to hear it from me. Are you okay?"

"No, as a matter of fact, I'm not," she said, and I believed her. The poor girl looked as though she were about to burst out into tears at any second.

"I didn't realize you two were that close," I said.

"We weren't, not really. I should have said something yesterday. I knew I was making a mistake, but I couldn't bring myself to do it, and now look what's happened." Her voice was dead and wooden, and I felt her pain from whatever was clearly haunting her.

"What's going on, Emma? You know you can always talk to me."

"Suzanne, I might know who did it," she admitted, "only I didn't tell anybody."

"Tell me," I said, forgetting about my coffee and donut for the moment, which was saying a lot, at least for me.

"Two days ago, I heard a ruckus going on next door at the construction site. It was such a beautiful morning that I had the windows open, and I could hear more than I bargained for. Two men were arguing in back, and from what I overheard, it was a real blowout."

"Did you recognize either voice?" I asked her.

"One of them was Mike, but I didn't know the other one," she said. "It was too early for anyone to be working, so I had to wonder if they'd met there on purpose out of sight. I peeked out back and got a quick look at them both, but I couldn't describe the other man to save my life. He was average in just about every way."

"What were they arguing about?"

"Money and business," Emma admitted. "The stranger told Mike that if he didn't back off, there was going to be trouble. I wanted to tell someone when I found out that Mike had been attacked, but I couldn't identify who he was arguing with, so what was the point?"

"You need to tell Chief Grant," I said as I reached for my cell phone.

"Suzanne, he's not going to be awake at this hour."

She was probably right. "Okay, fine, but when we open, we're going to call him. I'll do it with you, but he needs to be told. Agreed?"

"I guess I don't have much choice, do I?" she asked. "He's going to be really angry with me, isn't he?"

I knew that Chief Grant wasn't going to be all that happy about not getting the information sooner, but I wasn't about to tell Emma that. "Don't sweat it. The important thing is that you're going to tell him now."

"I hope you're right," she said.

"And you honestly have no idea who he was fighting with?"

"I told you, I didn't recognize the voice," she said, and I could hear her begin to whimper a bit. I knew that I needed to back off, at least until we made that phone call to the police chief, so I decided to drop it for the moment, with one last caveat.

"If you think of anything else, and I mean anything at all, tell me," I instructed her.

"I will. I'm so sorry, Suzanne."

"It's going to be okay," I told her just as the timer went off. I wasn't sure that was true, but it was all I could think to say to her. I just hoped that whoever had been arguing with the contractor so soon before he'd been attacked hadn't noticed the open windows at Donut Hearts. If he had, and if he'd been the one who had killed Mike Masters, he might just decide to come back and make sure there were no loose threads, which meant that he had to get rid of Emma, or even me, for that matter.

We were just about to open for the day, and I found myself dreading the telephone call we were about to make. I knew the police chief would be awake now. When he was working on a murder investigation, he kept hours like Jake did, and that meant being up well before the sun to get started on the day. Emma was clearly upset about it as well. She'd been distant the rest of the morning, and we'd had very few conversations in the course of our preparations.

"We need a sign," I told her suddenly.

"For what?" she asked.

"The donut sampling we talked about earlier, remember?"

"Oh, yes. Of course," she said as she wrote and decorated an announcement on the whiteboard we kept on hand for just such occasions. After she was finished, she asked, "How does that look?"

"I think it's perfect," I said. The donut she'd drawn looked so realistic it made me want to take a bite, and the inviting font she'd used was a sure way to get my customers' attention.

I looked up to see someone waiting to get into the shop before I opened the door. It was a face I hadn't seen in ages, and I offered him a smile. "Let's wait to call the chief until after I talk to an old friend first," I told her.

Emma, clearly relieved by the momentary reprieve, said, "Honestly, I don't care if we wait until we close." It was the happiest she'd sounded since she'd confessed to me what she'd overheard, but the joy went out of her the instant she glanced at the door herself.

"Suzanne, that's the man!"

"What man?" I asked her as I headed over to open the shop for that day.

"The man who was arguing with Mike Masters," she said, the fear and panic thick in her voice.

How was that even possible? The man waiting to get in was named Harry Duncan, and he owned a construction company all the way over in Talbot's Landing. What on earth had he been fighting with Mike

Masters about? Then I remembered Willis's comment about Masters cheating a builder out of this job, and it all started to make sense. That still didn't explain what Harry was doing at my donut shop, though. I didn't have the slightest idea why he would be paying me a visit, but I had a feeling that I was about to find out. Maybe I should have called the police chief right away, but I knew Harry, and I figured he had the right to tell his own side of the story before I called the cops on him.

"Harry, what are you doing here?" I asked him as I opened the door and let him in.

"I have some business with the guy working next door, so I thought I'd pop in and say hi to you first," he said. "How are you doing, Suzanne?"

"I've been better," I admitted. "What do you need to speak with Mike Masters about?"

"You know him? Listen, I don't want to air my dirty laundry in front of anybody else, you know? I just need to straighten some things out with him and to apologize for some of the things I said in the heat of the moment. I understand I owe you from before, but this doesn't concern you."

"Actually, it does, Harry," I said. "Mike died from his injuries yesterday afternoon after he was attacked the night before."

"He's dead? What happened?" Harry asked me incredulously.

"Someone hit him on the head with a hammer and then nailed him to a wall," I said.

"Are you telling me that somebody did that on *purpose*?" Harry asked as he slumped against the table. "I don't even know why I'm all that surprised. Mike brought trouble with him wherever he went."

"You were fighting with him a few days ago," I reminded Harry as I saw Emma go to the softball bat. I tried to shake her off, but she was determined. At least she kept it under the counter until we might need it.

"We were arguing, not fighting," he said with a frown.

"What's the difference?" Emma asked him in a curt voice.

"An argument uses words; a fight uses fists," he said. "I never laid a hand on the man, and that's the truth."

"What were you arguing about?" I asked him.

"He was trying to steal my business," Harry said in disgust. "Nobody wanted him, even at his cut-rate prices, but it still made me mad enough to drive over here and have a word or two with him. I swear that's all it was. I yelled at him, he yelled right back, and I took off. I didn't figure I'd have to warn him again. Mike always was a bit of a coward. He used to work for me until I had to fire him."

"Why did you do that?" I asked him.

"I couldn't trust him, and besides that, he just wasn't a very nice guy." Almost as an afterthought he added, "I know I shouldn't speak bad about people who are dead, but it's true. He bullied anyone he thought would take it and he cowered from folks who he suspected would fight back. That's spineless where I stand, whether the man is dead or alive."

"Harry, you don't have to answer this, but do you have an alibi for the night and the morning of the murder?"

He frowned. "I don't have anything to hide," he said. "I was in Myrtle Beach with my new girlfriend. She was in the car when we stopped here to warn Masters to back off, and we drove straight to the beach right after. I just got back late last night, and I came by first thing this morning to have another word with Mike. I was a little rough on him, and Shelly made me, er, she suggested that I make things right with him. I'm trying to be a better man, you know? When my wife found out that I'd been fooling around on her, she dumped me, and I couldn't blame her. I was a bad husband, but I'm working hard at being a better man. Do you believe in second chances, Suzanne?"

"Sometimes, if whoever is getting them takes them seriously," I said, thinking about my ex-husband, Max, and how hard he'd worked to change since his betrayal.

"Well, I'm taking this as serious as a heart attack," he said. "I can't believe Masters is dead. Now I won't have a chance to make amends."

"Yeah, I feel bad for you," I said, trying not to let too much sarcasm show through my voice.

"I know there's more at stake here than my feelings," he admitted. "I guess I'd better go by the police station and talk to your chief while I'm in town."

"You'd really do that?" I asked him.

"I'm kind of surprised you didn't tell him about me yourself," he answered. "That was a classy thing to do, Suzanne."

I wasn't about to tell him that if I'd known it was him, I would have called the police the second I'd found out. After all, he didn't need to know everything.

As I saw movement outside the shop, I said, "You know, you're in luck. Here come the chief and my husband right now."

As Jake and Chief Grant came into the donut shop, I braced myself for exactly how I was going to bring them up to speed on everything I'd learned that morning. Hopefully it would take the sting out of Emma's confession, especially if they could prove that Harry was in another state when the attack had happened.

"Chief, Jake," I told them as I stepped between them and Harry. "This is Harry Duncan, and he's got a few things to tell you."

Both men looked a bit guarded, but the chief said calmly, "Go ahead, Mr. Duncan. We're listening."

Twenty minutes later, Harry was gone. I'd had to wave off a few customers while he'd been telling his side of the story inside my shop, and there had been more than one surprised expression when they saw that the OPEN sign was turned out and yet they couldn't get their treats for the day.

I was going to have to give away more than just peach-raspberry donut samples to keep my customers happy, but I was more than willing to do it.

"What did you two come by for in the first place, anyway?" I asked Jake as the chief spoke in whispers on his cell phone.

"Believe it or not, we wanted a donut," he said with a grin. "These peach-raspberry ones are good. When did you decide to start making them?"

"This morning," I admitted. "Emma and I decided that we needed a change of pace." My assistant had left us all as soon as she could manage it and was now no doubt up to her elbows in hot, soapy water. The chief had taken the news of her failure to share information pretty well, only pausing to admonish her lightly to never do it again.

"I hope you don't mind me saying so, but they need something," he said after taking another bite.

"What can I say? Just like me, they are a work in progress," I admitted.

"I like the way you've turned out just fine," he answered with a smile.

"You have to say that. You're my husband," I told him.

"No, that's why I get to say it."

The chief got off the phone and walked back over to us. "He was at the beach, all right. There was a fire alarm in the middle of the night, and the manager remembers what an odd pair Harry and his girlfriend made."

"Why, was he that much older than she was?" I asked.

"No, but he was quite a bit plainer. The manager wasn't sure if Harry was rich or some kind of hypnotist, but he swore that Harry's girlfriend was way out of his league."

Jake touched my shoulder lightly. "I know just how he feels."

The chief grinned at that. "As a matter of fact, so do I. Most of us are with women better than we deserve, aren't we?"

"What can I say?" I asked them with a grin. "We ladies like a project."

"Thank goodness for that," the chief said. "Anyway, your friend Harry is in the clear."

"That's good to know. He hasn't always been the nicest man in the world, but at least he's trying to do better."

"I'm the first one to give him credit for that," the chief said. "Anyway, if we can get a donut or two apiece and some coffee, then we'll be on our way."

"What are you two up to this morning?" I asked as I filled their orders.

"Fighting crime and keeping the streets safe," Jake said with a grin.

"Yeah, what he said," the chief answered. It was clear he enjoyed having Jake with him, even if it was only on a temporary basis, and I knew that my husband enjoyed it, too. When he wasn't working on a consulting job somewhere else, he was always ready to pitch in at home, and April Springs was better for it.

"Stay safe, gentlemen," I said as I made change from the money the chief had given me.

"Hey, you gave me too much back," he protested when he counted it.

"I only charged you for what you had. My husband can have anything he wants here free of charge, and if you weren't such a stickler, so could you," I told him.

"Sorry. It's just the way I'm wired," the chief said.

"I hear what you're saying, but it doesn't mean that I'm ever going to stop trying," I told him with a grin.

"I can't fault you for that," the chief said as he headed for the door.

Jake smiled at me on his way out, and I turned back to the business at hand, at least the current business anyway.

I was in full-on donut-shop mode at the moment, but I knew that in a few hours, I'd have my investigating hat back on. Someone needed to figure out who had attacked and ultimately killed Mike Masters, and they needed to do it soon. Every hour we delayed was another hour folks would spend gossiping that Gabby Williams might have done it, and if the damage went on for too long, we might be too late to ever salvage what was left of her reputation.

Chapter 13

DURING A LULL IN MY customers, I looked out the front window and saw the same beat-up old van I'd spotted the day before drive past the donut shop. In a few seconds, it turned around and passed by again, but then I saw it start to pull over in front of ReNEWed. This needed to be investigated.

"Emma, can you watch the front for a few minutes?"

"Sure thing," she said as she came out of the kitchen, drying her hands on a towel. "What's up?"

"I just want to stretch my legs," I lied. I didn't really want to pull her into my investigation if I didn't have to, at least not any more than she already was, given who her father was.

"Take your time," she said as she started wiping down a counter I'd just cleaned. I thought about mentioning it to her, but what could another cleaning hurt?

I walked outside to find that the police tape was no longer across the front of the construction site, and two men who looked familiar to me were getting out of the van.

"You two work here on the construction site, don't you?" I asked them.

"We used to, didn't we, Manny?" the short and heavyset man in his forties asked the other man.

"Until th.....e old b....at f....ired us, anyway, Stu," the thinner and younger man stammered.

"Just because our boss got hisself killed, we have to be the ones who pay for it," Stu said.

I noticed a bottle of whiskey in Manny's hand, and he didn't even try to hide it in a plain brown paper bag as he took a substantial swallow.

"If you were fired, then why are you here?" I asked them.

"Came to get our tools," Stu said.

"Yeah, *our* t.....ools," Manny echoed. "You ain't with the p.....olice, are you?"

"Me? No, I'm just a donutmaker," I said.

They looked pleased by their play on words about tools, and I was pretty sure that anything they were about to take had once belonged to Mike Masters, not them. Still, who knew the contractor better than the men who worked for him? Maybe it was fortunate that I'd seen them.

"What did you think of your boss?" I asked them.

"He was better than most, but that's not saying much," Stu said with a shrug.

"Yeah, th....at's t.....rue," Manny answered, and then for some unexplained reason he started to giggle. "Not saying m....uch at all."

Stu looked unhappy with his partner's state of inebriation. "You're drunk."

"Am not," Manny said with a stupid grin on his face.

"Are too," Stu answered. "Anyway, we just came to get what's rightfully ours, and then we'll get out of your way."

Manny took another long swig, and then, noticing that the bottle was empty, he chucked it into the small dumpster that was sitting out front. "Th.....at w....as g....one qu...ick."

"Come on, Manny. Let's grab our stuff and get out of here," Stu said. "We need to get you sobered up."

"Wh....at f....un is th....at?" Manny asked with another stupid grin.

"Believe it or not, life doesn't *all* have to be fun," Stu answered.

"Should either one of you be driving?" I asked them, concerned for the folks of April Springs.

"Ma'am, I haven't had a drop to drink in six years and thirty-one days," Stu said. A reformed alcoholic I'd known once had been able to quote every day of his sobriety, so I had a hunch that Stu wasn't unfamiliar with AA. Good for him.

"Th.....at b...ottle w......as all m....ine," Manny said proudly. "G.....etting f....ired w.....as f....ine by m....e."

"Stop lying to the woman, Manny," Stu said.

"M....ake m.....e," Manny said with a grin.

They disappeared into the building, and I pulled out my cell phone as I walked back next door. Jake answered on the first ring. "Are you close by?" I asked him.

"We're at the chief's office," he admitted.

"You might want to get over to ReNEWed pronto," I said. "The two men who worked with Masters are over there even as we speak, looting the place."

"That's good to know, because we've been looking for them since yesterday morning," Jake said. "Thanks," he added, and before I could say anything else, he hung up the phone.

I went inside and relieved Emma of the front, and not three minutes later, I peeked out the front window and saw the squad car pull in behind the van, making it impossible for them to escape without driving through the police cruiser. Jake saw me looking out and gave me a quick thumbs-up as he followed the chief onto the property. Fifteen minutes and four customers later, I saw Chief Grant and Jake head back to the car without the construction crew. My husband paused before getting in the passenger seat and turned then shrugged in my direction before he got in. Had it been a dead end after all? I was an amateur, and I didn't mind admitting it, but I thought that lead might pan out. I put my vigil on pause every time I had a customer, so I must have missed it when Manny and Stu left. Whether they had tools with them or not I couldn't say, but I was going to have to mention their presence to Grace when we got together in an hour. She had agreed to meet me at quarter after eleven, and I hoped that the cash register balanced out with the report.

That was probably the only chance that I was going to be ready on time.

It was forty-five minutes before we were due to close for the day when one of my suspects stormed up to the Donut Hearts entrance, and I couldn't imagine why she looked so upset.

Then again, maybe I knew exactly why after all.

"Did you give the police my name?" Regina Davis demanded as she threw open the front door.

"Hi, Regina. How are you?" I asked, giving her my brightest fake smile. "It's a beautiful day out there, isn't it?"

"It was better before the cops came knocking at my door this morning before work," she said, clearly fuming.

"That had to be better than having them come by the scrapyard," I said. "What would your father think about that?"

"I'm living back home for the moment," she snapped. "He heard exactly what happened."

"Didn't he know that you were dating Mike Masters?" I asked her, taking a step back from her. The anger absolutely radiated off of her, and I was suddenly glad that our softball bat was in its proper place after all.

"What I do on my own time is none of his business, or yours either, Suzanne!"

I took a deep breath, and then I told her calmly, "I'm sorry to burst your bubble, Regina, but I didn't share your name with anybody: not the police, not my husband, and not the newspaper publisher either."

Her gaze narrowed for a second before she spoke again. "Why should I believe you?"

"Frankly, I don't care if you believe me or not," I said. "I'm glad that you're here, though. We never had a chance to ask you where you were the night before and the early morning when Mike was attacked."

"I was home." She pouted.

"Will your father tell us the same thing we ask him?" I asked her.

"He wouldn't know. Dad was gone that night," she said.

"Where was he?" Could Regina's *father* have made the attack on the contractor when he found out he was dating his daughter? I hadn't even considered the possibility, but now that it had come to my attention, it had to be worth considering.

"He didn't tell me where he'd been, and I didn't ask. If you know what's good for you, I wouldn't talk to him. The man doesn't like people prying into his life any more than I do."

"I'm sorry to hear that, but I may just have to take my chances with him," I said.

Regina took a few steps forward, and I could see that she was so angry with me that she was having trouble keeping her temper in check. "Don't do it," she said softly.

"Are you *threatening* me, Regina? You should know that I don't respond to that kind of intimidation tactic."

"I'm not threatening you, Suzanne; I'm just giving you a heads-up," she said.

Emma spoke from behind me, and until that moment, I'd been so focused on Regina that I hadn't even heard her join us. "Is everything all right out here, Suzanne? Don't forget, the police chief will be by any second to get that order."

Regina frowned for an instant before turning and leaving without saying another word.

"Really? What does Chief Grant want?" I asked her.

"He's not necessarily coming by immediately, but I know for a fact that he could be back here pretty quickly if we call him," she answered with a grin.

"You saw Jake and him drive up earlier, didn't you? I'm guessing you didn't believe my cover story about stretching my legs."

"I don't mind. I knew we had customers that you couldn't talk in front of, so I figured it was some kind of code. I peeked outside to see what was going on, and when you came back in, I ducked in back and propped open the back door so I could hear what was going on out-side."

"What exactly did you overhear?" I asked her.

She frowned a moment before speaking. "Honestly, not much," she admitted. "There was something about tools, and then 'public intoxica-tion' got batted around, but that was about it. What was going on over there, Suzanne? What did they want with Manny and Stu?" Of course Emma would know them. I was certain they'd visited her at the shop every day that I was gone.

"They came by to collect their tools after Gabby fired them. I was worried they were drinking way too early in the morning, so I called Jake and the police chief to give them a heads-up. It was all pretty inno-cent, at least on my end."

"You don't think they had something to do with Mike's murder, do you?" she asked me.

"That depends. Is my assistant, Emma Blake, asking, or does the newspaper publisher's daughter want to know?"

She thought about that for a second before answering. "I withdraw the question," she finally answered with a grin. "Honestly, I don't want to know the answer. After all, what I don't know, I can't spill to my dad."

"Fair enough," I said with a smile of my own. "How many donuts do we have left?"

"Forty-nine, if you can believe it," she answered with a frown. "We made way too many donuts this morning."

"Well, at least it's better than fifty," I responded. "We have a little less than half an hour left. Who knows? Maybe we'll get lucky and sell them all."

We didn't.

Not another customer came in for the rest of our shift, and it ap-peared that we'd be tossing a great many donuts today.

And then it hit me.

It would give Grace and me a perfect excuse to make up for the food the DeAngelis women had so graciously supplied us with the day before, and while we were in Union Square, maybe we could speak with Jillian Christie again. I had a feeling that there was more to her story than we'd heard so far, and I felt as though we needed to pressure her for a better answer about that black eye than her story about running into a door.

At least it was a plan, which was more than I'd had when the day had started. Investigations like ours worked that way sometimes. There were times when things seemed to fall into place with very little effort on my part, but those were rare occasions indeed. Most of them were like this one, where we had to scratch and claw for every clue, every suspect, every alibi, only to find most of them vanish in a puff of smoke. Just once, I'd like the killer to confess after hearing our first question, but I knew that was unrealistic. I believed that whoever had ultimately killed Mike Masters hadn't meant to. If they had, what had been the point of nailing him up and leaving him with a pulse? No, Mike's treatment struck me as a punishment for his behavior, a lesson he would never forget, and things had somehow gone too far. On television and in the movies, they made it look easy to hit someone over the head hard enough to knock them out but not kill them, but I knew that wasn't true. There was a fine line between assault and homicide, and someone had crossed it with the contractor.

I had a hunch that somewhere in our list of suspects we had the inadvertent killer.

The only question was, which one was it? Was it one of the spurned women, one of his employees, or perhaps a contractor rival? Then again, Regina's father might have had the misguided belief that he was defending his little girl's honor, though I knew that ship had sailed while we'd all still been in high school.

At least the list was manageable at that point. We had:

Regina Davis, one of Masters's girlfriends;

Garry Davis, Regina's father;

Jillian Christie, another girlfriend, this one in Union Square;

Manny, one of his employees;

And Stu, the other.

The only name I refused to put on my list was Gabby's.

She probably deserved to go on it, but I just couldn't bring myself to put it there. If Gabby *had* killed Mike Masters, either by accident or by design, someone else was going to have to figure that out and deal with it.

I could usually distance myself somewhat from the cases I worked to solve, but I could never bring myself to go after a friend.

I just hoped that it didn't come to that.

Chapter 14

"PERFECT TIMING," I told Grace as she walked into the donut shop. I'd been waiting for her for seven minutes, which was a nice change of pace. I loved it when everything worked out, and I'd sent Emma on her way so she could go to class. "Are you ready?"

"I didn't think you'd be finished this early," she apologized. "Sorry about that."

"No worries," I told her.

"What are we going to do with all of those?" she asked me as she pointed to the four boxes stuffed full of donuts.

"I thought we'd go by Napoli's first thing and pay down our debt a little bit," I answered with a grin.

"Suzanne, you didn't make extra donuts on purpose today just for Angelica, did you?"

"No, these were the result of an honest mistake of overestimating my customers' desires on a given day," I admitted. "At least it's better than running out. I hate when that happens."

"How many donuts are there?" she asked.

"Forty-nine," I told her. "Do you think it's too many?"

"For a party? No. For five women? Maybe. They freeze, don't they?"

"Yes, but they aren't nearly as good as they are when they're fresh," I admitted. "Should we cut back on what we take them?"

Grace shook her head. "You've got them, so let's deliver the entire lot. After all, Angelica asked for it by refusing to keep your money yesterday."

"These aren't meant to be a punishment, Grace," I reminded her. "I'm just trying to repay her for all of the food she's given me. It's true that I do want to work something out with her about how we charge each other for our goodies, but I want to be nice about it. Do you really think she's going to believe that there is an ulterior motive to this?"

"Probably not. With any luck, she'll take them in the spirit they are being given," Grace said. "Suzanne, I shouldn't have said anything. Don't overthink this, okay?"

"I'll do what I can, but I'm not making any promises," I said. "Let's take these out to the Jeep and head back to Union Square."

"What about lunch? I purposely didn't eat so we could grab a bite at the diner before we got started sleuthing."

"I suppose we *could* do that," I admitted.

"But you'd rather deliver these while they're still fresh," Grace finished the thought for me. "I get it. Let's go."

"Maybe you're right. We have to eat something, and I don't want to take advantage of Angelica's good nature any more than I already have lately."

"How many donuts did you say there were?" she asked.

"Forty-nine," I replied.

"So, if we bring her forty-six, she wouldn't be expecting more," Grace said.

I had to laugh. "Are you honestly proposing that we have donuts for lunch?"

"Well, *you* can have *donut* in the singular. I figure I should get the other two."

"Why is that?"

"It just makes sense, doesn't it? I'm willing to bet that you've already had more than one bite of one already today, or am I wrong?"

"No, it's true, but I ate those sampling a new recipe we're trying," I justified.

"Calories don't care," she said happily. "I can't wait to dig into these."

"Why don't you pick yours first, and then I can reseal the boxes," I told her.

I opened all four boxes and grabbed a to-go bag. When I got back, she was still trying to decide which ones she wanted. I snatched an apple-cinnamon cake donut while Grace selected an old-fashioned cake and a plain blueberry cake. "I thought you'd go for something like a double chocolate bomb or a triple strawberry frosted one," I said.

"Normally I would, but those are both too messy to eat in the Jeep, especially the way you drive," she explained with a hint of laughter in her voice.

"That's a fair point," I replied as I retaped the boxes. "Are you ready?"

"Let's hit the road," she said.

After I'd brought Grace up to speed on what had happened that morning and long past when our personal selection of donuts was gone, she wiped her hands on a napkin and said, "As much as I enjoyed that, I'm afraid that I'm going to need something more substantial for lunch."

"Me too. Just consider that the first course," I told her. "We can tell Angelica that we already had lunch, but she doesn't have to know that we're going to eat something else, too."

"The things we do for friendship," Grace said.

"It's why we're investigating this murder," I told her. "I know you and Gabby don't always see eye to eye, so I really appreciate you pitching in."

"We both know that Gabby is a challenge for most people," Grace reminded me, "but honestly, I just like hanging out with you. So, where do things stand at the moment?"

"I was thinking about that before you came by," I told her. "The way I see it, we have a handful of legitimate suspects left on our list."

"Regina and Jillian have to be right up there," she said.

"They are, and the two stooges who worked for Masters need to be there as well."

"Is there anyone else on it?" she asked.

"Garry Davis," I said.

"Regina's dad," Grace echoed. After pausing for a few moments, she asked gently, "Is there anyone else you think should go on our list?"

"No, not that I can think of," I answered quickly and perhaps a bit curtly.

After another long pause, Grace said, "Listen, I'm not saying she did it, but her name has to at least be on our roster of suspects, and you know it."

"Grace, if Gabby killed Mike Masters, whether on purpose or by accident, then the police chief is going to have to deal with it, because she's not even on my radar."

"Despite everything that we know?" she asked me softly. She was treading on thin ice, and she fully realized it. I believed in my friends no matter what, and Grace had to know that better than most.

"I don't want to even entertain the possibility," I said.

"Okay then, let's move on," Grace said, dropping it. "It's not like we have a shortage of suspects without her."

"That's true," I said. "Since we're going to be in Union Square anyway, I'd like to take another run at Jillian Christie. I'll trade you dollars to donuts that she got that black eye from Masters."

"No deal," Grace said. "What makes you think she'll admit it to us, though?"

"Maybe we'll see if Tianna could go with us," I suggested in a fit of sudden inspiration. "I have a feeling that Jillian might be a lot more willing to talk to us if her friend is there, too."

"Do you think she can get away from the restaurant to help us, even assuming that she's willing to join us in ganging up on her friend?"

"We're looking for the truth, not a scapegoat to pin this on," I told her. "Tianna wants to protect Jillian, so I have a feeling she'll jump at the chance."

"I hope you're right," Grace said as we entered the town limits of Union Square. The drive always felt as though it were cut in half when I had my best friend with me, and the miles just flew by.

As I pulled in back of the restaurant, I grabbed a few boxes while Grace collected the rest.

It was time to make good and give a little as a change of pace.

"Twice in two days. We're honored," Sophia said as we walked into the busy kitchen. She was hard at work, but she took the time to stop and wave to us as she reigned over the prep area as though she was born for it, and she grinned mightily when she saw what we were carrying. "Are those what I think they are?" she asked as she instantly dropped what she was doing and headed straight for us.

"Donuts!" Antonia said as she abandoned her station and rushed over to join us, too.

Maria wasn't far behind her sisters as she came into the kitchen from the dining area and asked, "Did someone say donuts?"

"Help yourself, ladies," I said as Grace and I put our boxes down on an empty table. "Where's your mom?"

"She's off running one of those mysterious errands she's been having lately," Sophia explained. "Tianna will be back here in a heartbeat, or I don't know my sister." Sophia grabbed the double chocolate bomb and ate a third of it in one bite. "Man, that's amazing." She looked at me quizzically and asked, "Not that I'm complaining, but you didn't make these just for us, did you? We honestly didn't mean to put you under an obligation to supply us with donuts just because we shared a little food with you yesterday."

"Sophia, are you honestly trying to discourage Suzanne from sharing her treats with us? That's a little hypocritical, wouldn't you say?" Antonia asked.

Sophia ignored her sister and kept her focus on me. "Suzanne? I'd love an answer to my question." She had her mother's focus and intensity, and I could feel the heat of her interest in my answer.

"These were left over from today's run," I told her honestly. "We needed to come to Union Square anyway, so I thought it might be a nice treat for you all. If I was wrong or I overstepped my bounds, I'd be happy to take them back with me." That was an outright lie.

"Try getting out the door with these," Maria said with a grin. "If you do, you're going to have a fight on your hands. If my sister doesn't want them, I'll take them all."

"Not without me," Antonia said after polishing off her donut and going for another. "If we can give Suzanne food, then she has every right to return the favor."

Sophia grabbed another donut and laughed. "Okay, I give in. It's a good thing that I can eat and cook at the same time."

"That's certainly an underrated skill set in my book," I said with a smile.

Sophia seemed to accept that, and then she said, "At least let me make you both lunch while you're here."

"Thanks, but we already ate," I said. It was one of the hardest semi-lies I'd ever told in my life. If they could bottle the aromas coming out of that kitchen and turn it into perfume or aftershave, it would be the most popular scent on the market.

Tianna looked through the boxes and then asked, "No double chocolate bombs?"

"You're too late," Sophia said with a grin. "I already got it."

"That's what I get for being conscientious and doing my job," she said. "Hey, here's a chocolate-covered cherry cake donut hiding under the paper."

"I didn't see that one," Sophia protested.

"That's an absolute shame," Tianna said as she took a big bite of the donut and smiled. "Wow, that's absolutely amazing."

"You're just plain cruel. You know that, don't you?" Sophia asked her.

"Here, I was just teasing," Tianna said as she offered the unfinished donut to her sister. "Take a bite. It's really great."

"You don't have to ask me twice," Sophia said as she bit the donut in her sister's hand, nearly nipping the skin.

"Hey, watch my fingers," Tianna said with a smile.

"Then keep them away from my donut," Sophia replied as she finished swallowing the substantial bite. "Thanks, T. You always were my favorite sister."

"Hey, I heard that," Maria said in protest as she looked up from the donut selection.

"Feed me treats, and maybe you'll move up in the rankings, too," Sophia said.

"Naw, I think I can live with things the way they stand now. Ooh, strawberry," she said as she pounced on one.

Tianna walked over to us and pulled me away from the group. "You're in town to see Jillian, aren't you?" she asked me softly.

"We are," I said. I looked at Grace, who nodded her approval for being excluded. It allowed her to distract the others while Tianna and I had ourselves a little chat. Grace knew that I'd tell her everything we discussed later, and while it wasn't ideal, it was probably going to be the best we could do, given the circumstances.

"Well, I'm sorry to be the one to tell you this, but you're not going to be able to find her, Suzanne."

"Why not?"

"Because she's in hiding, and nothing short of a warrant for her arrest is going to make her come out," Tianna answered somberly.

"Why is she hiding? Did she kill him, Tianna?" I asked her softly.

"No!" the eldest DeAngelis daughter protested. It had been loud enough to get everyone else's attention, but they weren't willing to interrupt us, at least for the moment. I knew the daughters were close to me, but if they had to run me over to get to one of their sisters, they wouldn't hesitate to do it, and what was more, I was okay with that.

After all, Grace would do the same thing if I was in trouble. It kind of came with the territory. In a softer voice, Tianna began again. "She knows how it looks, Suzanne, and she doesn't want to go to jail. She didn't kill Mike Masters, and that's the truth."

"I hate to even ask this, but how can you be so sure?" I asked her gently.

"Let me ask you something in return. Why aren't you going after Gabby Williams?" she countered. "You aren't, are you? Don't lie to me."

"We're not, and that's certainly a fair point. What did Jillian tell you?"

Tianna thought about that and then said, "Give me one second. I need to make a phone call." She stepped outside to make it, but I stayed right where I was. We weren't finished yet, at least I hoped we weren't, and I didn't want to give the other DeAngelis daughters an excuse to join the conversation. A minute later, Tianna came back in. "Okay, Jillian's given me permission to tell you everything."

"I'd really rather hear it directly from her, if it's all the same to you," I said firmly.

"I'm truly sorry, but this is the best I can do. You're going to have to take it or leave it."

"I suppose I'll just have to take it," I said.

"What Jillian told you yesterday was true. Well, at least most of it. She did dump Mike Masters, but it didn't go as smoothly as she presented it. She told him they were through, and he hit her! It wasn't the first time, but she swore to herself that it would be the last. She took her grandfather's old pistol and shoved it into Mike Masters's face. She told him that she'd kill him if he ever came near her again, and I honestly believe that she meant it from the way she told me about it, but he immediately backed up and ran for his truck. She said his face was white with fear, and she didn't think she'd have any more trouble with him. That's when she spotted a man walking quickly away from the scene with his bulldog. He had most likely witnessed the entire ugly conversation, and

Jillian's been waiting for the cops to come knocking on her door every second since. She can't just wait around for that to happen."

"She needs to go to the police and tell them her side of the story," I told Tianna. "If she doesn't want to talk to the chief of police here, I'm sure Jake and Chief Grant will help her get through this. Tianna, if she's innocent, she doesn't have anything to be afraid of." I wished that I could be one hundred percent of that being true. I sadly believed that innocent people did go to jail sometimes, but this was hardly the time or circumstance to bring it up.

"I can try to talk her into it, but I don't think she'll go for it," Tianna said. "Anyway, there's no sense in you going off looking for her. *I'm* not even sure where she is right now, and I'm about the best friend she's got these days."

"Okay, I appreciate you trusting me," I said. "If Jillian decides that she wants to talk to me later, give her my number." I scribbled down two cell phone numbers on a nearby piece of paper and handed it to her. "The top one's mine, and the other one is Jake's number if she'd rather talk to him. Tianna, you know my husband. He's one of the good guys."

"I know that," she said. "Thanks for understanding."

"Hey, we're all just doing our best for the folks we care about," I said, which was the entire and unvarnished truth. I wanted to protect Gabby just as much as Tianna was looking out for Jillian. That was what friendship was all about. It was easy to stand by someone's side when things were rosy. It was only when trouble hit that true friends stepped up and showed their real worth. "We'll be in touch," I said as I touched her shoulder lightly.

"Find the real killer, Suzanne," Tianna urged me.

"We're doing our best," I said. "Coming, Grace?"

"I am," she said as she turned toward me.

"What's that?" I asked when I saw a bag in her hand.

"I tried to say no," Grace explained helplessly.

"It's a little snack in case you get hungry later," Sophia said. "Thank you for the donuts. They were amazing."

Maria grinned and gave me two thumbs up as well.

I wanted to protest the never-ending cycle of free food when I realized that it was something I was going to have to deal with later with Angelica. It wasn't an argument I wanted to have with any of her daughters, that was certain.

Still, we'd have to work something out before too long.

I couldn't live with the constant state of imbalance between us, and there had to be something we could do so that we could both live with the results.

I wasn't at all sure what that might be at the moment, but in the meantime, Grace and I still had work to do.

Chapter 15

"MR. WILLIS, DO YOU have a second?" I asked the bail bondsman we'd met the day before as we walked into his office.

"You two are in the clear, if that's what you're worried about. And it's Willis. Just Willis."

"Excellent, Willis. We aren't here about that."

"Do the police know who broke in next door?" Grace asked him.

"The official line is that they are working on multiple theories, which proves to me that they don't know a thing," he answered with a smile.

"If you were to guess, who would you say might have done it?" I asked him.

He seemed to consider the question for a moment before answering. "I'd say it was either personal or professional."

"Wow, that really narrows it down," Grace answered with a grin.

I wasn't exactly sure that teasing the man was the way to go, but evidently Grace read him better than I did today. "That's a fair point. Let's see. I saw a few women come and go over the past few weeks, and none of them ever seemed all that happy with him. Then again, a contractor from Maple Hollow came by last week and told Masters that he'd see him in court."

"Are you sure he wasn't from Talbot's Landing?" I asked, thinking that he might be talking about Harry.

"The truck said Moorefield Construction, Maple Hollow, North Carolina," Willis said. "I have an eye for detail, and I don't get things wrong." He seemed more put off by me than he was with Grace at the moment, though she'd goaded him more than I had, at least in my opinion.

"She just means that we ran across someone from Talbot's Landing who had a beef with Mike Masters, too," Grace explained.

"I'm guessing you could line up folks who didn't like him out front and reach Cheap Cheeps from here," he answered. "Have you two ever been there, by the way? It has a bunch of the weirdest stuff for sale that you could imagine."

"We're both big fans," I said. "What about Masters's employees?"

"Are you talking about the idiot twins?" he asked with disdain. "Yeah, they weren't exactly happy with the way their boss treated them, based on the arguments I heard next door. These walls are as thin as paper."

"What exactly did they argue about?" I asked him.

"Evidently Masters had a habit of paying late, and less than he owed," Willis said. "He also made fun of the one who stutters all the time. The guy was a real jerk, to be honest with you."

"Could you see either one of them attacking their boss by nailing him to the wall?" I asked.

Willis frowned. "That's hard to say. Manny's a drunk and a bum, but I doubt he'd have the courage to face down his boss. Besides, I know for a fact that he didn't do it."

"How could you possibly know that?" I asked him. Was crossing a name off our list really going to be that easy? It had been known to happen, but certainly not all that often.

"He was in jail sleeping one off the night Masters was attacked," Willis said. "I know he didn't get out until nine a.m., because that's when I got him out."

"How about Stu?" I asked.

"No, he wasn't in the drunk tank," Willis said. "As a matter of fact, I don't think I ever saw him take a single drink from Manny."

That added up to what Stu had told us about his sobriety. "Do you think he might have been capable of doing it?" I pushed.

"You never know," the bondsman said with a shrug. "Stu kind of keeps to himself. He and Manny are tight. He treats him more like a little brother than he does a fellow worker."

"Do you know of anybody *besides* the women in Masters's life, local contractors, or the guys he worked for who might have had a beef with him?" I asked.

Willis looked at me curiously. "You two are digging into this, aren't you?"

"We are," I readily admitted. "Our friend is a suspect in the case, and we have no intention of standing by and watching her take the fall," I told him, stretching the point to include Grace. She and Gabby had an uneasy truce, but Grace really was doing this out of friendship, just not necessarily with Gabby Williams.

"So you're trying to figure out who did it so you can clear your pal," he said as he frowned. "You two should be careful. There are a lot of bad guys out there. Believe me, I've seen things that would make your blood run cold."

"Thanks for the advice," I told him, not wanting to admit that this wasn't the first time Grace and I had dug into murder. After all, he meant well, and under the gruff exterior was clearly a man with a good heart.

"There's no way I can talk you out of this, is there? The truth of it is that Mike Masters wasn't worth the effort. Excuse me for being so blunt."

"We'll watch our backs, but we really don't have much choice," I told him.

Willis frowned for a moment, and then he reached across his desk and pulled out two business cards. As he handed each of us one, he said, "If you get into trouble and you need some help, call me. I don't care if it's day or night. I'll come on the run."

I smiled at him. "We appreciate that very much, but I'm pretty sure we won't be taking you up on your offer."

He just shrugged. "That's your call, but you have my number, just in case."

Grace said, "Thanks so much," as a woman who looked rough as a cob burst into the office, fuming.

She shouted at Willis, "They arrested Vic again, Willis!"

"Settle down, Carla. I'll be right with you."

"They can't keep doing this," she said loudly.

"If he keeps driving without a license and they keep catching him, they surely can, and they will. You need to keep Vic off the road."

"You're more than welcome to try. I'm about ready to give up on him and let him sit in there until he comes to his senses," she said as she slumped down onto a chair.

"We won't keep you any longer," I said quickly. "Thanks again, for everything," I said as I waved his card in the air.

Carla perked up for a second and looked at me. "Don't shop around. Willis is the best there is."

"I don't doubt it for one second," I said as Grace and I exited.

Once we were back in my Jeep, I pulled out my cell phone and got Moorefield Construction's phone number. As I dialed it, I put my phone on speaker. "Is this Mr. Moorefield?" I asked when a man answered.

"It is. What can I do for you? We're booked solid for the next three months, but if you'd like, we can try to work you in."

I sincerely doubted that was true, but I gave him points for at least *trying* to look as though he was in demand. "I'm calling about Mike Masters," I said.

His tone went from pleasant and obliging to downright angry in a heartbeat. "I'm not dropping the suit, so tell your client that he's either going to pay me what he owes me, or I'll own every piece of equipment he has."

"I'm not an attorney," I said, and before he could ask me who I was, I asked, "When was the last time you spoke with him?"

"It was when I told him I was suing him a few weeks ago," the contractor said. "If you aren't his lawyer, then who are you?"

I decided to ignore the question. "Mr. Moorefield, Mr. Masters was murdered yesterday."

He didn't even pause. "Is he really trying to get away with not paying me by claiming to be dead? The nerve of that guy. He's probably sitting in some bar laughing even as we speak."

"I found the body," I said, which was true enough as far as it went. "I'm afraid he really is dead."

"Blast it all, now I'll *never* get paid," he fumed. "This is the worst thing that could have happened to me."

"To be fair, it wasn't so great for him, either," I said, and I saw Grace trying not to laugh. This man was clearly so self-centered that all he cared about was himself.

"I guess you're right at that. What happened? Did someone finally get tired of his lies and decide to shut him up for good?" This man didn't have an ounce of compassion, and I somehow felt myself feeling a little sorry for Mike Masters, which took some doing.

"That's what we're trying to determine," I said as officiously as I could manage. "Where were you two nights ago between the hours of eight p.m. and four a.m.?"

"I had my kids with me. I've got custody during the week, and my wife gets them on weekends. I have an old lady next door stay with them while I'm at work, but in the evenings, they are all mine. The thing is that my son has special needs, and I can't leave him alone for more than two or three minutes at a time. He's the joy of my life, and I couldn't love him more if I had a gun to my head, but it's a lot of work. He's worth it, though. You should see that boy smile! It lights up the whole room." Hearing the man talk about his son made me wonder if I'd judged him too harshly and too soon. It was clear that he loved his son.

"How's your daughter?" I asked him, curious about their relationship.

"She's just as amazing in her own way. My wife and I couldn't make it work between us, but we made some beautiful kids together." He paused and then asked, "Why am I telling you all of this? Are you a cop or something?"

"I'm something," I said. "Thanks for your time."

"Sure," he said, and then he hung up on me.

"So, he's off our list almost as quickly as he got on it," Grace said. "Were you as surprised as I was to hear the tenderness in his voice when he talked about his kids after the way our conversation started?"

"People aren't always what they seem," I said. "Whatever beef he had with Masters, I don't think he tried to settle it with a hammer and a nail gun."

"Then it's time to move on," Grace agreed.

My stomach rumbled, since one donut was not my idea of lunch. "Have you peeked inside that bag Sophia gave us?"

"No, I thought we were standing on our principles and refusing any more free food from the DeAngelis women," Grace answered with a grin.

"We probably should, but there's no reason to let good food go to waste, either," I said. "Don't you think we should at least see what it is?"

"It's the right thing to do," Grace said as she reached into the bag and pulled out two individually wrapped packages.

She handed one to me, and I tore it open. "It's a chicken parmesan sandwich," I said happily. Even though it was room temperature and not heated, I knew that it would be delightful. "What did you get?"

"It looks to be the other half of your sandwich," she said with a smile.

"This was all one big sandwich?" I asked incredulously.

"Would you expect anything less from Napoli's?" she asked me. "Should we eat these here or go someplace else?"

"Let's move on," I said. "I don't particularly want to see Willis and Carla when they come out. Have you ever seen a more defeated woman in your life?"

"She's clearly had a hard time of it," Grace said. "I wonder why she stays if she's that unhappy with him."

"People put up with a lot worse than that in the name of love," I answered.

"I suppose so," she answered.

I pulled into the nearly full parking lot of Cheap Cheeps and turned off the engine.

"We're eating here?" Grace asked.

"It's as good a place as any," I said as I took my first bite of my sandwich. It was delicious: the coating perfect and the chicken juicy, the bread fresh, the lettuce crispy. Grace joined me, and before I knew it, both of our sandwiches were gone.

"Suzanne, no offense, but that's what I call a lunch. As much as I love your donuts, that was exactly what I needed."

"Why on earth should I be offended by that?" I asked her as I wadded up my now-empty wrapper and shoved it back into the bag. "I've got to figure out a way to make things more equitable with Angelica. There is no way she's not getting cheated the way things are working now. What am I going to do, Grace?"

"Do you want my advice?" she asked.

"Of course I do. Frankly, I'm at a loss."

"I'd stick to your guns and insist on paying full price," she said.

"I've already tried that though, remember?" I asked.

"Yes, but you didn't tell her the second part of your deal. If she refuses to let you pay for what you get, you're going to have to stop going to Napoli's, and what's more, you're going to have to mean it. This can't be an idle bluff, Suzanne. She has to see that you are dead serious about it, and if she refuses, you have to walk away and wait for her to contact you. I'm willing to bet that she won't go more than a few days with things that uncomfortable between you."

"You know my husband is going to kill me if this doesn't work, right?" I asked her.

"*Jake*? You're concerned about *him*? Suzanne, you should worry more about *me*. If I have to give up my favorite place to eat because of you, I might bite the hand that's not feeding me."

"I'll make sure it's resolved one way or the other," I said. I was going to have to be firm, even if it meant risking hurting Angelica's feelings, but it had to be done. Just having a plan made me feel better, though. "What's next?"

"I don't have a clue," she admitted. "Who's still on our suspect list?"

"We have Regina, her dad, Jillian, and Stu on it as of right now," I told her.

"But still no Gabby?"

"No Gabby," I said firmly.

"Then let's go talk to one of them. We can't find Jillian at the moment, so that leaves Regina, Garry, and Stu."

"Since two of our three suspects work at the same place, let's go back to the scrapyard then," I said.

"We should get mileage for all of the trips we're making between Union Square and April Springs," she answered as I put the Jeep in gear and headed back toward home.

"We're working for free, remember? Who would we even charge?"

"Gabby?" she asked.

"Sure. Why not?"

Grace looked at me oddly. "Seriously? You'd really ask her for money to help her?"

"Well, it was *your* idea to charge someone. I think it's only right that you're the one who brings it up the next time we see her," I answered, knowing that there was no way on earth that Grace would ever mention anything like that to Gabby Williams. To be fair, there weren't many people who would. Gabby could be fierce to deal with even on her best days, and these most certainly weren't her best days, or anywhere near them, regardless of the good heart that I knew lurked just beneath the surface.

"How about if I chip in half for gas?" she suggested. "Shoot, if it saves me from talking to Gabby and asking her for money, I'll foot the entire bill myself."

"I appreciate it, but I'm good," I said with a laugh. "But thanks anyway."

"It'll still be there if you decide to change your mind," she said. "Which Davis should we go after first, then? Do you have any preferences?"

"Well, we've already had a pretty long chat with Regina," I said. "Let's speak with Garry."

"How are we going to do that without letting her know what we're up to?" Grace asked me.

"We bypass the office and go straight to the scrapyard," I suggested. "That's going to be our best bet to get him alone."

"That sounds like a plan to me," she said, and we made our way back home so we could speak with two of our last four remaining suspects.

Chapter 16

"HEY, IS THAT REGINA?" Grace asked me as we neared the scrap-yard. She was pointing to a banged-up red Subaru that had to be at least as old as we were leaving the parking lot.

"It is! I wonder where she's going in such a hurry."

"I don't know, but let's find out. How quickly can you turn this thing around, Suzanne?"

"It's a Jeep," I said. "Just watch me. Grab your hat and hold onto something."

I found a patch of empty grass beside the road and barely slowed down as I did a quick U-turn and headed in the other direction.

"Take it easy. We want to get there alive, Suzanne," she reminded me.

"Hey, you asked, I delivered," I told her.

"You're a maniac. You know that, don't you?"

"So I've been told." I tried to stay a decent amount of space behind Regina, but if she hadn't been so intent on wherever it was she was going, I wouldn't have gotten away with tailing her. It wasn't like I was a seasoned pro at it or anything, though Jake had given me a few tips years ago. Just like he'd taught me, I tried to allow a couple of car lengths between us, and I didn't make any sudden moves, at least not after I'd turned around on a dime to follow her in the first place. It would have been easier if we'd had another car so she wouldn't no-tice me hanging back in her rearview mirror, but this didn't require a great deal of stealth. Wherever Regina was heading, she was going there with great purpose. In fact, I probably could have been close enough to bump her before she noticed me, but I kept at a safe distance anyway.

It suddenly dawned on me where she was heading as she took a sharp left turn. "You know where she's going, don't you?" I asked Grace as I sped up.

"I don't have a clue. How can you?"

"She's headed for Gabby Williams's house," I said, putting my foot on the gas. I didn't care about being caught now.

I needed to protect my friend.

Grace and I pulled in just behind Regina, thanks to the fact that my vehicle was relatively new, while hers hadn't been able to make that claim for decades. She was in a hurry though, and I nearly had to jump out before I could bring my Jeep to a complete stop.

"Regina!" I shouted as I jumped out and went after her.

It was clearly the first time she noticed that we were even there as Grace joined me in hot pursuit.

"What are you doing here?" she demanded, not even slowing down.

"That's what we're wondering about you," I yelled. "Stop right there."

"Suzanne, this is none of your business. Butt out!"

"That's what you think! I'm *making* it my business," I said angrily. I had no idea what she was doing there, but I suspected that it couldn't be good. It didn't appear that Regina was armed as far as I could tell, but the woman was intimidating enough even without wielding a weapon.

"Go away!" she shouted at me.

I was about to pull out my cell phone to call Jake when the worst thing that could happen occurred.

Gabby came out of the house to see what was going on.

"You've got a lot of nerve coming here," Gabby told Regina fiercely as she stormed toward her. Had my friend completely lost her mind? She'd been safe enough inside, but instead of staying there where Regina couldn't get to her, Gabby had left her sanctuary and confronted the woman face to face. Then I realized that she must have seen and heard us arguing! She'd come out to protect me!

If anything happened to her now, it would be on my shoulders.

I had to stop this before it escalated to the point of no return.

Racing up to them, I threw myself between the two women. "That's enough!" I said. My heart was pounding in my ears, and I was having trouble catching my breath, and to her credit, Grace was two steps behind me and closing in fast.

"Why are you here?" I asked Regina once I got my wind back.

"I came to apologize!" she shouted at me. "Why do you two keep harassing me? I saw that insane U-turn you did! What is your problem, Suzanne? I didn't do anything to you!"

I could swear she looked as though she was going to cry. Was it possible that *I* had intimidated *her*? In a split second, I looked at the situation from her point of view, and I could see that she had a point. I needed to get myself under control, and I had to do it now.

"Why are you apologizing?" Gabby asked her curiously.

"I didn't know you were seeing Mike, too," Regina said, her voice approaching a sob. "He told me that it was all business. Gabby, I don't do that to other women. I'm so sorry."

I wasn't sure that Gabby believed her at first, but from the look in Regina's eyes, there was very little doubt that what she was saying was true. It didn't mean that she hadn't killed Mike Masters, but I honestly believed that she hadn't known until the very end that he'd been seeing Gabby, too.

"It's not your fault," Gabby said, softening instantly. "He was good at telling women exactly what they wanted to hear. We never stood a chance."

"I should have known better," she said, and finally the tears broke loose.

"I should have, too," Gabby said. Then, to my shock and amazement, Gabby leaned forward and put her arms around Regina! This was not the Gabby Williams most of April Springs knew, prickly and mean spirited, but instead, it was clearly a woman who recognized another wounded spirit when she saw one. "Let's get you inside," she said as she noticed that Grace and I were standing there, staring at them both openmouthed. "You two can go," she told us dismissively as Regina began to follow her inside.

"Gabby, can I have a word with you first?" I asked.

"Stay right here," she told Regina. The woman looked nearly catatonic, so I doubted that she was going anywhere.

"What is it, Suzanne?" she asked as she approached me. Grace at least had the sense to take three steps back so we could chat in private.

"I still don't trust her," I said softly. "You need to be careful."

"She's brokenhearted, Suzanne. Can't you see that?" Gabby asked me.

"Yes, I believe that part of it, but what if she's upset because *she's* the one who killed him?" I asked softly.

"Even if she did, *I'm* not in any danger from her," Gabby reasoned.

"How can you be so sure?" I asked her. "I'm worried about you."

"I know you are, but I can handle this, Suzanne. It's going to be okay."

"I'm not leaving here until she goes," I insisted like some kind of petulant child. I didn't care. How would I feel if Regina did something to Gabby the moment we were gone? I'd never be able to forgive myself, and I knew that deep down, neither would Grace.

"I appreciate your offer, but she's not going to talk to me if you're both hovering around outside my house," Gabby said softly. "And right now, she desperately needs someone who is willing to listen to her."

"You've really changed, haven't you?" I asked.

"We all do sooner or later, or we die," she said. "Now go," she added as Regina started to stir and look around.

"Fine, but you need to call me the second she leaves," I made her promise.

"You worry too much," Gabby replied.

"Maybe I do, but it's the only way we're going to go." I wasn't bluffing, either.

"Fine. I will, but this is going to take a while."

"Call me every hour until she takes off, then," I insisted.

"I'm not sure how convenient that's going to be," Gabby said, clearly unhappy with my stubborn insistence to ensure her safety.

"Do you want to know something? I don't care," I answered flatly.

"Fine. I'll do it. Just go," she prodded us.

It was the best deal I was going to get, so I took it. "Come on, Grace. We're leaving."

She didn't question me at all. We walked back to my Jeep, and when I looked over my shoulder, I saw Gabby gently leading Regina inside her home. Thinking about Gabby's reaction to the situation, it amazed me how much people were capable of changing if they were only given the chance. Sure, the situation still might end badly for my friend, but she was following her heart and trying to help someone in obvious pain, so who was I to stop her?

"Can you believe that?" Grace asked me as we got back into my Jeep.

"Which part of it? Regina was scared of *me*."

"Yeah, I caught that too, but I'm talking about Gabby suddenly becoming Mother Theresa. It seemed a bit out of character for her, don't you think?"

"Grace, I've said all along that Gabby had a good heart. She just chose to show it to the rest of the world."

Grace nodded. "Well, I know that I for one am impressed. I'm not sure *I* would have done what she just did, given the circumstances."

"You would have done exactly the same thing, and we both know it," I told her as I headed back to the scrapyard. After all, we'd originally set out to speak with Garry Davis, and I saw no reason not to continue with that plan.

"Probably," she said. "Are we going to go talk with Garry now?"

"We are unless you have a better idea," I told her.

"No, I still think it's a sound course of action," she said.

"Then let's do it."

When we got to the scrapyard, we saw a worried Garry Davis on the phone. "If you see her, call me, okay? I'm going out of my mind with worry," he told whoever he was talking to. When he saw us, he said, "You'll have to come back later. My daughter's missing."

"We know where she went," I told him.

Garry Davis slumped down a bit as he hung up the phone. "She had an accident, didn't she? I knew she was driving too fast when she left here. I should have kept my mouth shut." He was a big man with enormous and powerful hands, but at the moment, he looked more like a little lost boy.

"She's fine," I told him quickly. "We left her with Gabby Williams."

"You did *what*?" he protested as he grabbed for his keys. "That's the *worst* place she could be right now."

I stepped between him and the door, and he barely slowed down. I had to talk fast or I was about to get run over. "Garry, Gabby is helping her! You need to leave them alone!"

The words rocked him back, stopping him as though he'd run full steam into a brick wall. "Gabby? Seriously?" was all he managed to croak out. "She turned to *her* and not *me*?"

"Sometimes a woman scorned needs another woman," Grace said softly.

"I thought I was doing her a favor doing what I did," he said dejectedly. "If I hadn't stepped in, he would have kept using her until there was nothing left."

Were we about to get a confession from a murderer?

Chapter 17

"WHAT ARE YOU SAYING, Garry?" I asked him as I saw Grace make a move to retrieve her cell phone. "Are you trying to tell us that you were the one who attacked Mike Masters at ReNEWed?"

"What? No! Of course not," he insisted. "All I did was talk to him. That was it. I never laid a hand on the man, and that's the truth."

"Tell us what happened," I prompted him softly.

"Two days ago, I found out what was going on, so I went to see that jerk in his office," Garry confessed. "Let's be clear about something. I never threatened to kill him, and I didn't do it."

"What happened when you spoke to him?" Grace asked him.

"He treated me like *I* was the one out of line!" the scrapyard owner said with disgust. "We both started yelling at each other, and I got out of there before I did something I knew that I'd regret later," he said. "I decided to take a walk around the block to cool off, and when I got back, I decided that I was ready to give it another shot. I needed to convince him to leave my daughter alone, one way or the other. Only he wasn't there when I got back."

"What did you do then?" I asked.

"I didn't realize that he was gone until I tried his front door. The lock must have been stuck or something, because it opened the second I grabbed it, so I stepped inside, but the place was empty. I almost left right then and there, and I know that's exactly what I should have done, but I had to get him to see that he couldn't mess with my daughter and get away with it."

"So you decided to trash his office instead," I said in a moment of inspiration.

Garry looked at me as though I was some kind of witch. "How did you know that? Were there cameras in there or something?"

"No, but we saw the results of your little tantrum," I told him. "If you ask me, anyone capable of doing something like that is also capable of beating a man in the head and stapling him up against a wall." I started to realize that Grace and I were in a precarious position at the moment. There might have been two of us against his one, but the man was huge, and it was clear enough that he had trouble controlling his temper.

"I didn't do it!" he shouted, and I started edging toward the door. We had to get out of there, and fast.

Grace had another question for him, though. "If you're telling us the truth, make us believe it," she insisted. "Do you have an alibi for that night?"

"Yeah," he said reluctantly, "but I'm not going to tell you about it."

"Even if it means we call the police and tell them that we think you might have been the one who attacked Mike Masters?" I asked as I pulled out my phone. He couldn't stop me from hitting a nine and two ones, so at least Jake would know what had happened to me.

"If I share that with you, will you promise not to tell Regina?" he asked, nearly pleading with us.

"Why can't she know?"

"Because I was in Charlotte with her mother," he admitted as he slumped into a chair.

"Why can't she know that?" I asked, holding off on dialing for backup just yet.

"I've been dating Barbara, that's my ex, for a few months now, but I'm not sure if it's going to stick this time around or not. We split up when Regina was a little girl, and every year for Christmas, all she'd ever ask Santa Claus for was us to get back together. It wrecked her, and what was worse was the fact that I knew it. Anyway, I ran into Barbara a few months ago, and we clicked, you know? Maybe we both needed the years apart to realize what we'd had was pretty good, or maybe we'd both grown up enough to see the other person for who they really were, flaws and all."

"Do you think Regina *still* wants you two to get back together?" I asked him. I hadn't had a great deal of sympathy for the man when I thought he'd been about to clobber us, but I could see that there was a softer and gentler side to him, too.

"Does that ever go away, wanting to see your folks back together?" Garry asked. "Anyway, I was staying with Barbara the night Masters was attacked. I didn't hear about it until I got back here the next morning."

"You know that we need to call your ex-wife and confirm it, right?" Grace asked.

"I don't want you doing that," Garry answered with a frown.

"We won't tell anyone we don't have to, including your daughter, but it's the only way we'll be able to tell the police that you have an alibi for the night of the attack. Or would you rather they come here and grill you about it while Regina is standing right beside you? It's your call," I told him, though I hoped that I'd presented it in a way that gave him every incentive to do it my way.

"Fine," he said as he took out his phone. "I'll call her."

"Give me her number instead," I told him.

Garry looked at me oddly. "You still don't believe me, do you?"

"Let's just say that I'd like to ask Barbara about where you were before you have a chance to warn her," I told him. "I'm not lying to you, Garry. If she confirms your story, then we're not going to tell anybody if we don't have to."

He grumbled a bit, but he finally gave me the number.

I put the phone on speaker after warning Garry not to talk, and a woman answered on the third ring. "I checked my caller ID, and I don't know you. Why are you calling me?"

"It's about Garry," I said.

Her voice was a shriek. "Did something happen to him? Is he dead? I never got to tell him that I loved him!"

I could see that he was about to say something when I gave him a glare that shut him down. He might have intimidated us, but evidently I had a little bark in me, too. "He's fine. Were you with him two nights ago?"

"Who is this?" she asked me.

"I'm leading an investigation into a man's murder," I said. It was true enough, though I might have failed to correct her in her natural assumption that this was an official investigation and not an amateur one.

"He was with me," she said hurriedly. "All night."

"Are you telling me the truth, or are you covering for him?" I asked her.

"I'm telling the truth," she snapped. "We ordered pizza at midnight just before the joint down the street closes, so they'll have a record of it. Garry had to order it because I was in the shower, and he paid for it with his debit card. That's all I'm going to say!"

She hung up on me before I had a chance to thank her for cooperating, and as I was putting my phone away, Garry Davis's phone rang.

"Yeah, it's okay. Calm down. I'm all right. I love you, too," he said. "Yeah, you're right. We've got a lot to talk about."

I looked at Grace and motioned her to the door.

"Let's give them some privacy," I said softly.

Once we were outside, Grace said, "I can't believe he's still trying to shelter his daughter at her age."

"I think it's kind of sweet he cares," I countered.

"Trashing Mike's office wasn't exactly the act of a gentle soul," she reminded me.

"No, you're right. Anyway, we can take his name off our list for now. That pizza delivery is too easy to check on, so for the moment, let's just assume that it will hold up and move on."

"Where does that leave us?" Grace asked as I started the Jeep and headed in toward town.

"We have alibis for Garry Davis and Manny the builder, but we still need them for Regina, Jillian, and Stu. If you ask me, *one* of them attacked Mike Masters and ended up killing him, even if they didn't mean to."

Just as I finished speaking, my cell phone rang. It was Gabby, and she sounded worn out when she spoke. "Regina just left here," she told me.

"Are you okay?"

"I'm fine, but wow, did Mike do a number on her. She's about to fall apart, but I think I got her together enough for her to at least make it home. She told me she's going to curl up on the couch once she gets there and not come back out for a month."

"What did you two talk about?" I asked.

"Suzanne, she didn't confess to killing him, if that's what you're asking," Gabby said sharply.

It was, but I couldn't exactly admit that now. "I just wanted to make sure that she was okay."

Gabby softened instantly. "She's not at the moment, but I have hope. Regina told me she was going to take a hard look at herself. Maybe the shock of Mike's death was what she needed to turn herself around."

There was something I needed to say, but I wasn't sure how to bring it up. Gabby must have sensed my hesitation. "What is it, Suzanne? What's on your mind?"

"I need to remind you of something. Gabby, just because she's falling apart doesn't mean that she *didn't* kill Mike," I told her.

"Don't you think I know that?" Gabby asked wearily. "I was careful."

"If you were to guess, do you think she might have done it?" I asked her.

Gabby took a long time to answer me. "To be honest with you, I wouldn't rule it out," she finally admitted.

"Thanks for being honest with me," I told her. "You sound beat, if you don't mind me saying so."

"I'm drained," she confessed. "Maybe I could use a little alone time myself. I think I'm going to take a hot shower and then have myself a bite to eat. One more thing, Suzanne."

"What's that?" I asked, preparing myself for another barb.

"Thank you for coming after her today. I know you were just trying to protect me, and I appreciate it. I might not always show it, but I feel the same way about you."

I was about to reply when she hung up. Gabby probably didn't want to hear anything sappy from me in response, but I was okay with that. We knew where we stood with each other, and I could live with the fact that she really didn't want to hear me affirm it.

"Regina's probably home by now," Grace said after I brought her up to speed. "Should we go over there and apply a little more pressure?"

"No, let's let her have a little time to get herself together," I said. "Grace, I know it might make perfect sense to push her when she's feeling vulnerable, but I just don't have the stomach for it, do you?" The woman's near-catatonic state was too fresh in my mind, and going after her now would make me feel like a bully. We were trying to find the contractor's killer, not drive a woman who very well could be innocent over the edge.

"I know exactly what you mean. I'm not sure that I could face that, either. Maybe that's why we'll never be able to turn pro, Suzanne. We're too soft. That just leaves Stu and Jillian on our list," Grace said.

"Well, we don't have any idea where Jillian might be, and Stu is probably somewhere in Union Square. Grace, I can't stand the thought of going there again today."

"Me either, and besides, we don't even know for sure that he lives there," she reminded me. "In fact, how would we even go about finding him?"

"I suppose it's too much to ask for him to be in the phone book," I said.

"Who has a phone book these days? Let me look him up online. What's his last name?" she asked me as she pulled out her cell phone.

It suddenly occurred to me that I didn't have a clue. "I have no idea."

"It's going to make it tougher narrowing it down from all of the other Stus in North Carolina," Grace said with a frown.

"I'd say that it was impossible," I told her.

"Of *course* it's impossible," she replied with a shrug. "Let me try something else." She tapped a few more keys on her phone as I sat there wondering what to do next. We were at another dead end, and until we could shake things loose, I didn't see where we could go until something else happened.

"I guess I shouldn't be surprised that Masters didn't have a website," she said in disgust.

"Did you honestly think that he would?" I asked her. "You saw the man's office. I doubt he even had email."

"How could anyone function in this day and age without an email account, let alone a man trying to run a business?" she asked me in wonder.

"Believe it or not, it happens," I said. We had a rudimentary site for Donut Hearts, but it wasn't much to speak of, and I'd put it up reluctantly. I was an old-fashioned gal in a world that seemed to keep getting more and more modern. In my opinion, there was something to be said for not being connected with everyone else on the planet in a world-wide web of entanglements. It was probably a simplistic point of view, but I was glad that it was one my husband shared with me. When we were together, the two of us enjoyed being disconnected from the rest of the world, but it probably helped that we not only loved each other, we liked each other, too.

"I get that," Grace said. "It looks like we're drawing a blank. I could always call Stephen and ask him for Stu's last name."

"I'd rather you didn't," I said. "I don't want our investigation interacting with the official one. Don't worry. We'll find him later."

"Okay, but what are we supposed to do in the meantime?"

My stomach grumbled a bit despite the delicious sandwich Grace and I had shared earlier from Napoli's.

"Well, we both have leftovers from last night. Why don't I drop you off at your place, and we can get started bright and early in the morning, if you're free again?"

"Don't you have to work?" she asked me.

"It's time for Emma and Sharon to take over for a few days," I told her. "Can you get away?"

"If I work tonight, I'll be free as a bird tomorrow," she said.

"I don't want you to have to do that."

"Suzanne, I'm volunteering. You'd better take me home now, though. I've got numbers to massage and calls to fake before I can go to bed."

I knew better than to ask her if she was serious. Sometimes not knowing what Grace had to do in order to make time to help me with my investigations was for the best for everyone.

"Are you going to be okay by yourself?" I asked her.

"I'll be fine," she said. "After I eat some of the leftovers, I'll be able to focus on work."

"Aren't you going to share any of it with Stephen?" I asked her. There had been plenty of food left over from our feast the night before to serve four more people.

"You're right. I should invite him over." In a soft voice, she called out, "Stephen, would you like to have dinner with me tonight? If I don't hear from you in five seconds, I'm going to keep it all for myself. One, two, three, four, five. Okay, understood. I take it you're too busy."

She then grinned at me and added, "You heard it yourself. I made the offer."

"I'm not sure I'd be able to testify to that in court," I answered with a smile.

"Then let's hope it doesn't come to that," she said with a grin of her own.

I drove to her house, but before she got out, she turned to me and said, "Suzanne, don't do any sleuthing without me."

"I'll try not to, but sometimes I just can't help myself," I said with a laugh.

"I get that. The things I can't help myself doing are too many to start listing right now. If anything comes up, call me. Otherwise, I'll see you bright and early at ten tomorrow morning."

"I was thinking about getting started at six," I told her.

"Nobody's going to be up then. Let's at least compromise a little bit and make it seven. Don't eat breakfast. We can start our day with a good meal at the Boxcar Grill."

"It's a date," I told her, and then I waved and made sure she got in the house safely before I drove the rest of the short distance to my place. It had been both a productive and frustrating day, but that wasn't all that unusual when I was working at solving a murder. All I could do was keep gathering more and more information until I was finally able to know in my heart who the guilty party was. Until then, at times, it felt as though I was just spinning my wheels, but at least a few good things had come from the day's investigation, and I decided that I should be happy enough with that.

Then I turned the last bend and saw two people sitting on my front porch, one an old friend and the other a suspect in the murder case I was currently working on.

Chapter 18

IT WAS JILLIAN AND Tianna, and at first glance, I couldn't tell which one of them was the worse for the wear.

They stood up as I parked and approached them. "What's up, ladies?" I asked them.

"Jillian needs to talk to you," Tianna told me, and then she turned to her friend. "Go on, tell her what you told me."

Jillian looked as though she wanted nothing more than to run off my porch into the woods, but she suddenly seemed to take strength from her friend's presence beside her.

"Go on. Tell her. This is important," Tianna urged her friend gently.

"I didn't kill Mike, and I can prove it," she finally said.

"Why would you be afraid to tell me that?" I asked her after I led them into the house.

"I don't know. I just want this to go away! What if whoever attacked him comes after me next?" she asked, the fear thick in her voice.

"Why would they do that? Do you know something that you shouldn't?" I asked her.

"No, I don't think so, but that's the thing, isn't it? The killer might not realize that! If they know that Mike and I were close, they might think I'm a loose end that needs to be tied up!"

"First of all, you said earlier that you could prove that you didn't do it," I said, trying to keep my voice calm. "Let's get into that before we start borrowing trouble. Tell me how you can do that."

"I was staying with a girlfriend and her boyfriend the night Mike was attacked. Shelly's guy didn't want me there, and he made it a point to tell me just that. He and Shelly started fighting about her friends always coming first, and she told him that I needed her. I tried to leave the second they started fighting, but she wouldn't let me! When Jeff, that's her boyfriend, realized that Shelly wasn't going to budge, he stormed out. I was so upset that I tried to leave again too, but Shelly wouldn't let me. She hid my car keys, she was so worried about me driving while I was upset. Anyway, Jeff was only gone a few minutes. He came back and tried to apologize, but Shelly wasn't very receptive. He must have spent hours trying to convince her that he cared about her until she finally relented. We were all together the entire time, and I didn't find out about what happened to Mike until the next morning."

"We need to call Shelly to confirm that," I said. I wasn't asking for permission, but I did want them to know what I had to do.

"Be my guest," Jillian said as she grabbed her phone and dialed the number from her list of contacts.

Shelly confirmed it quickly enough and even offered to put Jeff on the phone. Evidently they had patched things up, because he was still there with her. He agreed that they hadn't left each other's sight other than the few minutes he was outside. I ended with, "Don't go anywhere. You're going to be getting another call sometime in the next hour."

"Call us anytime. We'll be here," he said.

As I handed Jillian's phone back to her, she asked, "Why do you need to call them back? Didn't they just confirm that I was telling the truth?"

"It's not for me, it's for the police," I told her.

"The police?" she asked, the fear jumping back into her words. "Why do we have to get *them* involved in this?"

"Jillian, a man you were dating and just broke up with was murdered. Don't you think the police chief is going to want to know that you've got an alibi? That's assuming that you haven't told him already."

"I heard he was looking for me," she said hesitantly. "That's why I ran away."

"But you're innocent," I insisted. This woman was missing the entire point.

"That doesn't mean that they still wouldn't arrest me if they got it into their heads that I did it," she protested.

"My husband would *never* let that happen," I assured her.

Tianna said, "We need Jake."

"He's with the police chief," I said as I shrugged. "I'm afraid at this point, they're a package deal, kind of like Grace and me."

"Go ahead and call him, Suzanne," Tianna said.

"I'm not so sure about this," Jillian replied.

"I am. You can't keep living with this hanging over your head, not when we can clear it up with one more conversation. Come on, Jillian. This needs to happen, and it needs to happen right now."

She deflated a bit as she finally agreed, "I guess you're right. Go on, Suzanne. Call him."

"I will," I answered as I pulled out my cell phone.

"This isn't a great time," Jake said when he heard my voice. "We're trying to track one of our suspects down, and she's missing."

"If you're talking about Jillian Christie, she's sitting in our living room right now with Tianna DeAngelis."

"You're not kidding, are you?" he asked me, barely missing a beat.

"Not about this, I'm not. Can you come home?"

"Bring her over to the station, Suzanne," he said firmly.

"Hang on. I'll ask her." I put the phone to my shoulder and looked at Jillian. "He says he can't come here. We need to go over to the station."

"I don't want to do that," she protested.

"I'll go with you," Tianna said.

"I will too, if that helps," I volunteered.

"Fine. Whatever," she said after giving it a bit of thought. "We might as well get this over with. I know I can't keep dodging them forever, and the quicker they know that I didn't do it, the faster they can find the real killer."

"We're on our way," I told Jake.

"You're coming, too?"

"Yes. Jillian could use the company," I told him, and then softly I added, "Meet us outside, would you?"

"I can do that," he said.

We all drove over in Tianna's car. It was a two-door hatchback, and I was relegated to the back. My knees were in my chest the entire drive, and I was happy it was a short trip.

Jake met us outside and alone as promised. He looked at Jillian sympathetically and smiled at her. "Thanks for coming in, Jillian."

"You're welcome."

"What can we do for you?" he asked, and I suddenly realized that I'd forgotten to tell him that she had an alibi for the time of the assault/murder.

"I have an alibi!" she blurted out.

Jake nodded. "That's great news, and we'd love to hear it. Why don't you come back to the chief's office with me, and we can get this straightened out."

He moved to go inside, but Jillian stayed rooted to her spot. "I'm not going anywhere without them," she added as she pointed to us.

Jake didn't look at Tianna or me. He simply stared into Jillian's eyes as he said, "We'll take it easy on you, and we won't be long, but we need to do this part without them."

She looked uncertainly at me and then Tianna. I said, "You can trust Jake, Jillian. He's one of the good ones."

"You have to say that, Suzanne. He's your husband," Jillian protested softly. "Tianna? What should I do?"

"All I can tell you is that I trust Jake, and you can, too," she said without hesitation.

Jake nodded in our direction. "Thanks for the vote of confidence, ladies. We won't be long."

To Jillian's credit, though it was clear that she was terrified about the prospect of the coming interview, she followed Jake into the station, only stopping to look back at us once along the way.

"Is she going to be all right?" Tianna asked me a few minutes later after they were inside.

"I guarantee you that Jake will watch out for her," I said.

"I know he will, but I'm still worried about Jillian. I hope I did the right thing bringing her here to you."

"Tianna, you did the only thing you *could* do," I told her.

We stayed outside since the evening was nice, and I only had to fight back a few yawns, which fortunately Tianna didn't notice.

After a few more minutes, she asked me, "Do you think there's the slightest chance she was right?"

"About what?"

"That the killer might come after her next," Tianna said gravely.

"I can't imagine that happening," I said, hoping that it was true. "Why would they?"

"Everybody who ever met him knew that Mike Masters was a big blowhard," she said. "It's possible he told her something significant without her even realizing it at the time."

"If that were true, there would be a great many more people in danger than just your friend," I answered, "but if it would make you feel any better, why don't you invite her to stay with you for a few days?"

"Do you think that's all it's going to take to find the killer?" she asked me.

"I've got a hunch that it will be sooner rather than later," I told her.

"Why do you say that?"

I wasn't sure how much I wanted to share with her. Now that Jillian had an alibi, our investigation was down to just two people, Regina Davis and Stu. It was entirely possible that neither one of them killed the contractor, but I believed that we were on the right track and that one of them had committed the assault that had turned into murder.

"Call it an educated guess if you'd like. I might be wrong, but I'm not uncertain," I said, trying to add a slight smile to soften my words.

"I trust your guesses," Tianna said, "and so does my mother."

I thought about getting into my dilemma about paying for food with Tianna, but I never got the chance. The door to the police station opened, and Jillian walked out as though she'd just lost fifty pounds off her shoulders. "I'm free to go!" she said. "I can't believe how easy that was."

"I told you that it was the right thing to do," Tianna told her.

"Suzanne, your husband is amazing. He really took care of me."

"I told you that he would," I said, and then I glanced at Tianna. "What were you saying earlier?" I asked her as a prompt as I glanced toward her friend.

"Jillian, how would you like to come over to my place and stay with me a few days? It will be fun, and I think you could use a break from your regular routine."

"You're worried about the killer coming after me now too, aren't you?" she asked, the carefree look in her eyes suddenly dimming.

"No, I don't think it's going to happen, but why take any chances? We've been threatening to do this for years, so what better time than now to pull the trigger?"

"Are you sure you want me staying with you?" she asked her.

"I'm not just howling at the moon," Tianna said, and Jillian laughed. It must have been some sort of inside joke between them. Grace and I had plenty of those ourselves, and I was happy to know that Tianna had such a good friend herself.

"Then I won't, either," she said. Jillian then hugged me fiercely. "Thank you so much for helping me, Suzanne."

"Any friend of Tianna's is a friend of mine," I told her. "I'm glad I could be there for the both of you."

"So are we," Jillian said. "Come on, I'll give you a ride back to your cottage."

I shook my head. "Thanks for the offer, but it's an easy walk home from here," I told her.

Jillian looked around at the darkness that now surrounded us. "Are you sure? If anything happened to you, I'd never be able to forgive myself."

"I'm positive," I said. "Now scoot, you two. You've both had long days."

"More than you'll ever know," Tianna said. "Are you sure we can't give you a ride?"

If it was all the same to me, I'd never get into that back seat again willingly. "I'm going to be fine walking. It's a beautiful night, and there are plenty of folks still out and about."

"Okay, then," Tianna said. "Come on, Jillian. Let's swing by your apartment, pack you a bag, and go to my place."

"That sounds like a little bit of heaven to me," she admitted.

I watched them drive away and thought about going into the station to say hello to my husband, but then I decided to walk home after all.

I wasn't sure if it was because of the murder or the concern Jillian and Tianna had for me walking home alone, but I could swear that I heard footsteps in the park behind me as I cut behind the Boxcar Grill on my way to the cottage.

"Hello? Is anyone there?"

There was no response, which was what I'd expected, so I took a few more steps forward.

And then I heard the scuffling sound again, and what was worse, it was quite a bit closer to me this time.

Chapter 19

AND THEN I SPOTTED a squirrel rooting around for some last-second seeds or nuts before bedtime. I laughed nervously the instant I realized it, but that didn't keep me from hurrying home and locking the door behind me the second I was safely inside.

The women had been right about one thing.

Whoever had killed Mike Masters, inadvertently or not, was still on the loose, and I had to watch my step until someone caught the guilty party.

"Wow, I can't believe so many people get up this early on purpose," Grace said as she looked around at the packed Boxcar Grill the next morning.

"Are you kidding? This is late as far as I'm concerned," I said. We'd just finished our breakfasts and were ready to get started again as we walked to the front to pay our bill.

"How was your food, ladies?" Trish asked us.

"Delightful as always," I said.

"We aim to please," she answered as she gave us our change. "Will I see you both for lunch?"

"That's too far in the future for us to plan," I admitted.

"I'll give you credit for knowing what to do with a few days off," she said. "What are you two up to, as if I had to ask?" she added softly.

"You know, hanging out and stuff," I said evasively.

"Sure you are," Trish answered. "Good luck."

"Thanks," Grace replied before looking at me. "Suzanne, there's no use denying it. She knows what we're doing, and so does half of April Springs."

"I know, but I don't like admitting it out loud," I said.

"Sorry," Trish answered without an ounce of regret in her voice. "I didn't mean to blow your cover." In a louder voice she said, "Enjoy your day off doing nothing."

"That was smooth," I answered with a grin.

"Don't I just know it," Trish replied.

We were walking down the steps when we ran into a new acquaintance of ours. "Manny, what are you doing here?" I asked him.

"St...op sh.....outing," he said as he held his hands to his head.

"Are we a little bit hung over, perhaps?" Grace asked loudly as she leaned toward him.

He flinched from the verbal assault. "I d...on't kn....ow ab....out y....ou, b....ut I'm a l.....ot hung over. I've got a f......eeling th....is j....ob in....terview isn't g....oing to g.....o v....ery well."

"Are you really looking for work so soon?" I asked him.

"I've g.....ot to eat, d....on't I? N....ow th.....at M....ike's g....one, I d....on't have m....uch ch.....oice."

I looked around. "Where's your partner?"

He snorted. "He's l....eaving t....own. Af.....ter all w.....e've b.....een thr.....ough and he b.....ails on me. It's t....ough l.....osing your j....ob and your b....est fr....iend so cl....ose t.....ogether."

"I knew you were friends, but I didn't realize you were that close," I said.

"Yeah, w....e g....o w.....ay b.....ack. He's al.....ways had m....y b.....ack."

"Where's he going?" Grace asked.

"Atl....anta," he said.

"Do you happen to know where he lives right now?" I asked. If Stu was leaving town, I wanted one last shot at him.

"B....etween h....ere and M....aple H....ollow," he replied. "Th.....ere's a m....otel th....ere c....alled M.....ountain View, r....oom tw....elve."

"Thanks," I said. "Good luck on the interview," I said.

"Th...anks. I'll n.....eed it."

"Where are we going in such a rush, Suzanne?" Grace asked me as I blew past the speed limit on my way out of town.

"We need to talk to Stu again before he can leave town," I said.

"I wonder if Stephen and Jake know he's planning on skipping out," she said.

"I don't know, but I want to talk to him first. When we leave there, we can call them."

"You're the boss," she said.

"Don't you approve?" I asked her.

"I think it makes perfect sense, but it might cause some waves with the men in our lives," she replied.

"I can live with it if you can," I told her.

"You know me. I've never run away from a fight in my life."

"As a matter of fact, you usually run toward them," I answered with a smile.

"I can't deny it. Slow down, you're going to miss the turn."

I tapped the brakes and made the turn into the flea-bitten motel. It looked like a place where bedbugs went to die, and I wondered how desperate Stu must be to stay there. I couldn't blame him for moving, but I didn't want him going out of town, at least not until I could get an alibi from him.

His old van was parked in front of his room, and I noticed that some things were already inside it. It appeared that Manny had spoken the truth about him leaving.

"Going somewhere?" I asked Stu as we walked to the door of room twelve.

"What are you two doing here?" he snapped at us. "Haven't you two had enough of sticking your noses where they don't belong?"

"Is that any way to treat two old friends?" Grace asked him.

"I've only got one friend in this world, and his name is Manny."

"But you're leaving him behind, aren't you?" I asked him.

"I tried to get him to go with me," he answered with a shrug, "but he wants to stay here. This area has brought me nothing but trouble, and I'm leaving it in my rearview mirror, with or without him."

"That's fine, but we have one last question for you," I said. "Where were you the night your boss was assaulted?"

"That's none of your business," he said as he started loading his van again.

"Maybe not, but if you don't tell us, the police are going to want to know, and they aren't nearly as nice as we are when it comes to asking questions," I told him.

"I've got nothing to hide, so I'm not afraid of the cops," he said with a snort.

"Maybe you should be. What's the big deal, Stu? It's a simple question."

"Yeah, but the answer isn't. She's married, and I'm not going to get her in trouble."

"Just give us a name," Grace prodded. "That's all we need."

"That's a hard pass. I didn't kill my boss. That would have been stupid, especially since I'll never get paid for the last two weeks now. If you're looking for whoever attacked him, try Regina Davis. That woman has a temper a mile long, and Mike was really messing with her head. I can't tell you how many times I heard them going at it on the job site," he said. "Now get out of my way. I'm out of here as soon as I get some money a guy owes me, and he's supposed to come by any second."

"If you won't tell us who your alibi is, then you know that you'll just have to tell the police," I said. "Come on, Grace. Let's go."

Once we were out in the Jeep, Grace asked me, "Seriously? You're going to just let him off the hook?"

"No, I'm calling my husband," I said. "Let him deal with it."

Jake didn't answer, though.

I left him a message, and then I turned to Grace. "Try Chief Grant's number."

She did, and then frowned. "He's not answering, either."

"Leave him a message then," I told her.

After she did as I asked, she put her phone away. "So, do we stake Stu out and follow him?" she asked as she pointed in the direction of the man's van.

"No, there's nothing else we can do to stop him, and I'd still like to speak with Regina."

"Let's go, then," Grace said.

As a matter of fact, we weren't all that far from the scrapyard. I pulled the Jeep into the parking lot and found the place was devoid of customers, so at least there wouldn't be any witnesses to our upcoming questioning.

Regina was clearly upset about something when we walked in, and I wondered if we'd given her enough time to come to terms with what had happened.

"How are you doing this morning?" I asked her gently.

"I thought I was doing okay, but then I found something out that I just can't wrap my head around."

"Is it about Mike?" I asked her gently.

"No, Mike Masters is in my past. There's nothing I can do now about what happened between us. I've got to forget he was ever in my life and figure out what comes next."

"Then what's troubling you so much?"

"I didn't mean to eavesdrop, but the phone rang ten minutes ago, and I answered it right after my dad did. Evidently his cell phone was off, so she had to call on the landline."

"She?"

"My mother," Regina said in disgust. "Why was she calling him? I don't get it. I thought they couldn't stand each other, but you should have heard the way they were talking." She blushed a little as she described it.

"Maybe it's a good thing," I suggested.

"I don't think so. They were toxic around each other," Regina said. "If two people ever didn't belong together, it was my mother and father."

"So you don't *want* them to get back together?" I asked her. Garry had been so sure of it that it surprised me to hear Regina say otherwise.

"Maybe when I was a kid, but I know better now. She'll kill my father if that happens, and I'm not going to stand by and watch it happen. I've got to stop her." She suddenly grabbed her keys and headed for the door just as Garry came in the back way.

"Regina, wait! Let me explain!"

"I heard enough on the phone!" she shouted back as she ran out of the office.

"Where is she going?" Garry asked us heatedly.

"My guess is that she's heading to Charlotte to confront her mother," I told him. "Garry, she doesn't want you two to reconcile."

"What am I going to do?" he asked, and then he answered his own question. "I've got to stop her." As he raced for the door, he threw a set of keys at me. "Lock the place up for me. I've got to catch her while I still can."

I tried to stop him, but I couldn't do it.

"They're going to end up in a ditch somewhere if they don't slow down," Grace said as we watched them tear out of there. "What should we do?"

"What can we do? We need to lock up," I said.

"I've never been back here before," I said as we walked into the scrapyard and headed toward the rear gate. The acreage behind tall fences was cluttered with bent and twisted steel, aluminum, old tires, soda cans, and things I didn't recognize. Some of it had been separated into neat little bins, but most of it was strewn across the land in what appeared to be haphazard fashion to me. We locked the back gate and had just started walking back to the front when I saw someone appear near the entrance.

It was Stu, last name still a mystery, but that hardly seemed to matter at the moment.

He had a crazed look in his eyes and a gun in his hand.

It appeared that we had poked a killer once too often, and now we were going to pay for the mistake with our lives.

"Run!" I shouted at Grace as I took off among the piles of twisted steel.

Grace followed me, but then she decided at the last second to veer off in another direction. I stopped in my tracks. "What are you doing?"

"Keep going," she urged me on. "One of us needs to get out of this alive, and our odds double if we split up."

The last thing I wanted was to leave her side, but she was right. It would be too easy to pick us off if we were together. The only hope for one of us to get out alive was to separate, as much as it pained me to admit it. This thought process took less than a second as I continued on into the twisting maze of metal and debris and started up the incline of the hill behind me.

I decided my best bet was to work my way around him to the front gate. I knew that he couldn't wait where he was forever.

As I ran in a crouch, I pulled out my cell phone and called Jake again.

Still no answer.

I was about to dial 911 when I heard Stu shout, "I've got Grace, Suzanne. Come out, and I won't hurt either one of you."

I didn't believe him, but really, what choice did I have?

I wasn't about to sacrifice my friend's life just for a chance of making it to freedom on my own.

Even if it worked out that way, I'd never be able to look at myself in the mirror again.

No, this was going to be my last stand if that was what it took to save Grace's life.

Chapter 20

"DON'T DO IT, SUZANNE!" Grace shouted.

"Shut up or you're dead," I heard Stu reprimand her. I was actually closer to them than I realized. How could I save her? There were plenty of blunt instruments lying around that I could use as weapons, but he had a gun, and unless I could get close enough to club him from behind, they were all worthless. I had made it up onto the hill so I could see what was going on, and sure enough, down below me about fifty feet, I saw Stu and Grace.

He had the gun pressed to her side.

I had to do something!

And then I spotted a massive yellow excavator off to one side. One glance told me that I'd never be able to operate the complicated piece of machinery, but beside that was an old pickup truck with a snowplow blade attached to it. It most likely served as a way to move some of the scrap around the yard, but I needed it for something else.

I got in the cab and was relieved to find the keys in the ignition. I wondered if I could lift the plow's blade and use it as a shield from Stu's bullets, but I couldn't take the time to figure the controls out.

"You've got until the count of five," Stu said, "and then I'm going to kill her."

I heard Grace ask him, "Why did you kill your boss, Stu?"

"Does it matter? He picked on Manny one too many times. I stayed back on the site to tell him to knock it off, and he just laughed at me! People have been picking on his stutter all his life. I warned him about it. Masters pushed me, so I pushed him back. He figured out that I was the one who tipped Gabby off about his double-dealing life, and he was already mad at me! Maybe I shoved him a little harder than I had to, but I was mad, too. He hit his head, but he was breathing when I left him."

"Why did you nail him to the wall, though?" Grace asked.

"I thought he'd wake up and have time to think about what he'd done before somebody found him," he admitted. "I knew that I was through the second I shoved him, so I decided to teach him a little lesson while I was at it. I figured when he came to, he'd stay there until someone came along and helped him, but he wasn't my problem anymore. When nobody came and arrested me the next morning, I got curious, so I grabbed Manny and headed to the site like nothing happened. That's when I saw the police tape. I asked a cop what had happened, and he told me that Masters was in the hospital. I didn't shove him that hard!"

"Why did you hang around town after what happened?"

"Nobody would know that I was the one who did that to him until he came to," he said. "*If* he came to. I started to realize that if he did, I was going to go to jail, so I had to take matters into my hands. They didn't have any security on him at the hospital, and to be honest with you, it was easier than I thought it would be. All it took was a pillow for a minute or two, and my problems were over. At least I thought they were until you and your friend started nosing around asking questions."

"You killed him on purpose the second time?" she asked him incredulously as I took the truck out of gear.

It started to coast down the hill immediately.

I wasn't at all sure that my plan would work, but what choice did I have? If Grace and I were going to die, we were going to do it together.

Thankfully, she spotted the truck before he did. When Stu finally saw it, he lifted the gun to shoot at me. Grace could have run then, but she chose to stand her ground and fight him instead. I saw her slam her foot down on his, and the gun wavered as it barked out. He missed me with his first shot.

My element of surprise was gone, so I turned the engine on, and thank goodness it started right up.

The windshield took the bullet from his second shot, and I heard it whiz past six inches from my head!

I'd been right; the plow was too low to protect me, at least at this angle.

I jammed the accelerator down and barreled toward the killer and my friend. I was hoping and praying that Grace would take the opportunity to get away, but if she didn't, I was ready to crash the truck into a tall pile of old tires stacked beside them. If I lived through that, my plan was to get out and fight on the ground side by side with Grace.

The bullets kept flying my way, and I had to duck down to keep from being shot, but at least if he was shooting at me, he wasn't going after Grace.

In a split second, I knew that I had to slam on the brakes or I'd kill them both.

Only the brakes weren't any good, and I felt myself barreling even faster toward my best friend and the killer with no way to stop it.

Chapter 21

I DID THE ONLY THING I could think of.

I jerked the steering wheel at the last second and sent the truck sideways straight into the pile of tires.

Had Grace gotten away, or had she been buried in the debris along with Stu?

Chapter 22

"SUZANNE, ARE YOU ALL right?" Grace asked me as she pried the passenger-side door open. I wasn't entirely sure that it had worked even before the impact, but it was certainly not working all that well now.

"I'm okay," I said. "How about you?"

"I'm fine, but if you're all right, then why are you bleeding?"

I shrugged and looked into the rearview mirror. There was a trickle of blood coming from my forehead. "Don't worry about it. It's just a scratch."

"Hold this against it," she said as she handed me a clean handkerchief as I crawled out of the cab.

"Is he dead?" I asked, dreading the thought of killing someone again. It had happened before, and I still had nightmares about it. Was I about to add another set of bad memories into the mix?

"No, he's probably bruised and battered, but he's cussing you pretty hard," she said with a grin. "Most of the tires missed him, but a few have him pinned down, so he's not going anywhere anytime soon. You don't have to worry about him shooting at you anymore, either," she added as she held the gun up for me to see. "Suzanne Hart, that was either the bravest or the stupidest thing I've ever seen in my life."

"Can't it be a little bit of both? Are you really okay?"

"Besides a few sore ribs where he poked me with his gun, I'm just dandy," she answered with a grin. "Thanks for coming to my rescue."

"Don't give me too much credit. If you hadn't distracted him while he was shooting at me, I would be dead right now."

"So once again, we ended up saving each other," she answered as a squad car pulled up and joined us.

I nearly fell into my husband's arms when he got close enough.

"Are you okay?" he asked gently.

"I'm a little shaky, but I will be," I said.

The relief flooding through him was obvious as the chief made sure that Grace was unhurt as well. Another squad car arrived quickly, and two officers I knew got out. "Where is he?" the chief asked.

"Follow the sound of his voice," I said as I pointed to the scattered pile of tires.

As the officers dug him out, Jake said, "We need to get you to the hospital."

"It's nothing," I said.

"It doesn't look like nothing to me," he said, and then he glanced at the truck that I'd just wrecked. "Remind me not to let you drive either one of my trucks ever again." He said it with a grin, and I matched it with one of my own.

"That's not going to be a hard promise to keep," I told him. "Did you finally get our messages?"

"We did. My blood ran cold when you said that Stu was trying to kill you both! Sorry it took us so long to get here. We were at the motel looking for Stu," he admitted. "I had no idea the place was in a dead spot. Neither one of us could get signals on our phones."

"Well, you made it after all, and that's all that counts."

"A day late and a dollar short," he said. "Come on. Let's go." He turned to the chief. "Can I borrow your ride?"

"Be my guest," he said as he tossed Jake the keys to his cruiser. "We'll catch a ride back to the station later," he said.

I tossed him the scrapyard keys Garry had thrown me earlier. "Don't forget to lock up on your way out."

Chapter 23
Three Days Later

"ARE YOU SURE ABOUT this?" Jake asked me as I got up to go back into Napoli's kitchen after we'd finished our meal.

"I'm afraid that it's the only way. I need you to have my back on this, Jake."

He nodded, but I knew that he'd agreed to my plan with great reluctance. If my scheme didn't work, I was going to regret it for the rest of my life, but I didn't feel as though I really had any choice.

"Angelica, we need to talk," I said the moment I walked in back.

"Was there something wrong with your meal, Suzanne?" she asked, sensing my somber mood.

"I don't understand. That food was perfect," Sophia said with a puzzled look on her face.

"It was. I have no issue about that. It's the bill I'm not happy about."

"But you shouldn't have gotten a bill at all! Don't worry about a thing. I'll have a word with Tianna," she said as she started for the door.

"That's the problem, Angelica. If you don't start charging me full price for what I eat here, I won't ever be able to come back. Putting that sixty dollars back in my bag was a dirty trick. Honestly, I expected better from you than that."

Sophia took a step back, and as Antonia came through the kitchen door, her youngest sister waved her off. Antonia sized up the situation immediately and ducked back out to the dining room where it was safe.

"You don't mean that," Angelica said.

"Look at my face and tell me that I'm not serious," I said, not breaking my stare at all.

"Suzanne, this is simply something friends do for friends," she haltingly explained. "It's a family thing, and you are my family."

"And you and your daughters are mine, but let's face it. I eat here a lot more than you eat at Donut Hearts, and I can't have this continue. I'm sorry, Angelica. It's breaking my heart to do this, but I don't feel as though I have any other choice."

Grace had called me brave back at the scrapyard, but that had been nothing compared to the courage it took for me to turn my back and walk out of that kitchen.

Angelica didn't stop me either, and I felt my own heart breaking a little.

"Come on. We're leaving," I told Jake grimly.

"I'm sorry, Suzanne," he answered as he stood and joined me.

We were at the front door when Angelica came out, waving something in the air. "Aren't you forgetting something, Suzanne?"

"What's that?"

"It's your bill for tonight's dinner," she answered.

I ran toward her and hugged her fiercely. "I love you. You know that, right?"

"I do, and the feeling is mutual. I love you, too," she said.

Both of us were weeping now, but we quickly got our tears under control. Angelica looked around and saw that everyone dining there had been watching the exchange. "Don't let your food get cold on our account," she said with a firm smile pressed to her lips.

Everyone got the message immediately and turned back to their meals.

As Jake paid the bill in full, Angelica asked me, "Were you really going to just walk away from me and my daughters like that?"

"I didn't want to, but what choice did I have?"

"I can see that I was wrong." As she handed Jake his change, she said, "There's one condition, though."

"Hang on one second. We didn't agree to any conditions," I warned her.

"Let the woman talk, Suzanne," Jake urged me.

"I'm sorry. Go on, Angelica."

"When you're here and I'm trying out a new recipe, I hope you'll agree to continue to test it for me. I won't pay you for the work, but I'm not about to charge you for the privilege of tasting our experiments, either. That you must take or leave."

I was smart enough to realize that she needed at least that much from me, so I readily agreed. "Fine. You've got yourself a deal," I said as I hugged her again.

As I did, she whispered with glee into my ear, "Sophia and I have been dying to try some new recipes, so expect my call any day."

I had to laugh. Maybe I hadn't won the war, but it was at least a draw as far as I was concerned.

As Jake drove me home in his new old truck, I marveled at how an act that had begun defending a friend had transformed into murder. Stu's motive of standing up for Manny had been gallant enough, but it had led him down a dark path from which he'd never find his way into the light again.

I found myself thankful once again for the family and friends who had my back and never asked anything in return.

It was what made my life worth living, and I promised myself that I'd never take it for granted.

RECIPES

Cinnamon-Apple Baked Donuts

Like Suzanne, we enjoy baked donuts sometimes, and here's a good place to start if you'd like to try to make them yourself. You don't have to worry about dropping dough into hot oil if you bake your donuts, and they feel as though they are a tad bit healthier to me (whether they really are or not), but to be fair, I've burned my forearms pulling trays out of hot ovens as well as getting splashed a few times with piping-hot oil, so you have to be careful no matter how you choose to make your donuts.

It's worth the risk though, at least as far as I'm concerned, and my family would certainly agree!

Ingredients

2 packets (1/2 ounce) dry yeast

1/2 cup warm water

1/2 cup granulated sugar

1 cup applesauce

3 tablespoons butter, melted

2 teaspoons cinnamon

2 teaspoon nutmeg

1/2 teaspoon salt

2 eggs, lightly beaten

5 1/2 to 6 1/2 cups all-purpose flour

Topping

1/3 cup butter, melted

1/3 cup sugar

1 tablespoon cinnamon

Directions

In a large bowl, dissolve the yeast in warm water and let sit for 5 minutes.

After 5 minutes, add the sugar, applesauce, melted butter, cinnamon, nutmeg, salt, beaten eggs, and 3 cups of the flour all at one time to the mixture.

Beat this mixture at low speed with an electric mixer until combined, and then mix for another 2 minutes at medium speed.

Once that is finished, stir in the flour a cup at a time until it forms a soft dough.

Turn the dough onto a lightly floured surface and knead by hand about 5 minutes, or until it is smooth and elastic.

Place the dough into a lightly oiled clean bowl, cover, and let rise until doubled, approximately 1 hour.

Punch the dough down and place on a lightly floured board. Roll the dough to 1/2-inch thickness and cut out the donuts into sizes and shapes you desire.

Place the donut shapes, rounds and holes, onto a greased baking sheet, cover, and let rise again for approximately 30 minutes.

Preheat the oven for 425 degrees F and bake for 8 to 12 minutes, or until the donuts are golden brown.

Brush the tops of the donuts with melted butter and then dip the donuts in the sugar/cinnamon topping.

Makes 10 to 14 donuts, depending on the size and shape you choose.

Easy-Peasy Blueberry Delights

If you've been reading my recipes very long, you'll know that sometimes I like complicated instructions, and sometimes I just want a treat as quickly as possible. Hey, at least I'm not denying it! This is definitely from the easy category. I keep packets of muffin mix on hand at all times, and blueberry is my favorite, though I've enjoyed the cranberry muffin mix, too. You could even use plain mix, but I like a bit of a zip in my day, and these warm treats provide just that!

Ingredients

1 package blueberry (or flavor of your choice) muffin mix (7 ounces)

1/2 cup flour

1/2 cup buttermilk

1 egg, beaten

Fresh blueberries if you've got them, but frozen work, too.

Optional

1 tablespoon confectioners' sugar

Directions

Heat your canola oil to 350 degrees F.

While the oil is coming to temperature, in a large bowl, mix the flour into the muffin mix and then add the beaten egg and buttermilk.

Stir until incorporated, but try not to overstir the mix, and then add the blueberries last.

Drop teaspoon-sized bits of batter into the hot oil and fry for 4 minutes, turning halfway through, or until the donut bites are golden brown.

Drain and dust with powdered confectioners' sugar or eat plain.

Makes approximately 8 to 12 donuts, depending on the size drop you make.

Raisins and Oatmeal and Cranberry, Oh My! Donuts

This remains one of my favorite "loaded" donuts, and that's saying something. I've been accused of gilding the lily in the past, and with this recipe, I don't even try to deny it. My daughter calls these "kitchen sink" donuts, because I throw just about everything I have on hand into them. On occasion I've added other things as well, including chopped pieces of orange slice candy, several different kinds of nuts, and even candied fruit. If you can put it into a cookie, try it in your donut. Your only limitation is your imagination, but as always, I can't guarantee the results, so please go forward at your own risk!

P.S. My attorneys just advised me that the hyperbole above might be lost on some folks. There's not really any risk to this recipe other than maybe creating a not-so-perfect batch of donuts.

P.P.S. I don't really have any attorneys. I just made that last part up, but what do you expect from me? I make my living telling tall tales!

P.P.P.S. The donuts really are great if you follow my instructions above, and that's certainly no lie!

Ingredients

1/2 cup granulated white sugar

1 egg, beaten

1/2 cup whole milk (2% can be substituted)

2 tablespoons canola oil

1/2 teaspoon vanilla

1 cup all-purpose flour

1/2 teaspoon cinnamon

1 teaspoon baking powder

1/2 teaspoon baking soda

1/4 teaspoon salt

Additions

2 tablespoons oatmeal (old-fashioned, not quick)

2 tablespoons raisins

2 tablespoons dried cranberries

1 tablespoon flour

Optional

1 tablespoon confectioners' sugar

Directions

Start by heating enough canola oil to fry your donuts at 350 degrees F.

In a large bowl, start by adding the sugar to the beaten egg and then mixing it. Next add the milk, oil, and vanilla and stir the mixture.

In a separate bowl, sift the flour, cinnamon, baking powder, and salt together, holding out the oatmeal, raisins, and cranberries.

Fold the dry ingredients into the wet, and then add the oatmeal, raisins, and cranberries after coating them with a small amount of flour so they won't sink into the batter.

Drop teaspoon- to tablespoon-sized pieces of batter into the oil. Fry for 4 minutes, turning them halfway through, or until all sides are golden brown.

Drain on a rack over paper towels and dust with confectioners' sugar or eat as they are.

Makes 8 to 16 donuts, depending on how generous you are with your drops of batter.

If you enjoy Jessica Beck Mysteries and you would like to be notified when the next book is being released, please visit our website at jessicabeckmysteries.net for valuable information about Jessica's books, and sign up for her new-releases-only mail blast.

Your email address will not be shared, sold, bartered, traded, broadcast, or disclosed in any way. There will be no spam from us, just a friendly reminder when the latest book is being released, and of course, you can drop out at any time.

Other Books by Jessica Beck

The Donut Mysteries
Glazed Murder
Fatally Frosted
Sinister Sprinkles
Evil Éclairs
Tragic Toppings
Killer Crullers
Drop Dead Chocolate
Powdered Peril
Illegally Iced
Deadly Donuts
Assault and Batter
Sweet Suspects
Deep Fried Homicide
Custard Crime
Lemon Larceny
Bad Bites
Old Fashioned Crooks
Dangerous Dough
Troubled Treats
Sugar Coated Sins
Criminal Crumbs
Vanilla Vices
Raspberry Revenge
Fugitive Filling
Devil's Food Defense
Pumpkin Pleas
Floured Felonies
Mixed Malice

Tasty Trials
Baked Books
Cranberry Crimes
Boston Cream Bribes
Cherry Filled Charges
Scary Sweets
Cocoa Crush
Pastry Penalties
Apple Stuffed Alibies
Perjury Proof
Caramel Canvas
Dark Drizzles
Counterfeit Confections
Measured Mayhem
Blended Bribes
Sifted Sentences
Dusted Discoveries
Nasty Knead
Rigged Rising
Donut Despair
Whisked Warnings
The Classic Diner Mysteries
A Chili Death
A Deadly Beef
A Killer Cake
A Baked Ham
A Bad Egg
A Real Pickle
A Burned Biscuit
The Ghost Cat Cozy Mysteries
Ghost Cat: Midnight Paws
Ghost Cat 2: Bid for Midnight

JESSICA BECK

The Cast Iron Cooking Mysteries
Cast Iron Will
Cast Iron Conviction
Cast Iron Alibi
Cast Iron Motive
Cast Iron Suspicion
Nonfiction
The Donut Mysteries Cookbook

Printed in the USA
CPSIA information can be obtained
at www.ICGtesting.com
LVHW012151130823
755142LV00038B/581